TOMBSTONE

Every town has a story. Tombstone has a legend.

From HOLLYWOOD PICTURES ANDREW G. VAJNA presents

A SEAN DANIEL JAMES JACKS CINERGI Production

KURT RUSSELL VAL KILMER

"TOMBSTONE"

MICHAEL BIEHN POWERS BOOTHE ROBERT BURKE DANA DELANY

SAM ELLIOTT STEPHEN LANG JOANNA PACULA BILL PAXTON

JASON PRIESTLEY MICHAEL ROOKER JON TENNEY

BILLY ZANE and CHARLTON HESTON Music by BRUCE BROUGHTON

Editors FRANK J. URIOSTE, A.C.E. ROBERTO SILVI HARVEY ROSENSTOCK, A.C.E.

Production Designer CATHERINE HARDWICKE Director of Photography WILLIAM A. FRAKER, A.S.C.

Associate Producers WILLIAM A. FRAKER and JOHN FASANO

Executive Producers BUZZ FEITSHANS ANDREW G. VAJNA Written by KEVIN JARRE

Produced by JAMES JACKS SEAN DANIEL and BOB MISIOROWSKI

Directed by GEORGE P. COSMATOS

DOLBY STEREO IN SELECTED THEATRES

Distributed by BUENA VISTA PICTURES DISTRIBUTION, INC.
© Cinergi Productions N.V. and Cinergi Productions Inc. All Rights Reserved.

These credits were not contractual and were subject to a WGA arbitration at the time of printing.

CINERGI

HOLLYWOOD PICTURES

TOMBSTONE

**A novel by Giles Tippette
Based upon the screenplay by
Kevin Jarre**

B
BERKLEY BOOKS, NEW YORK

If you purchased this book without a cover, you should be aware that this book is stolen property. It was reported as "unsold and destroyed" to the publisher, and neither the author nor the publisher has received any payment for this "stripped book."

TOMBSTONE

A Berkley Book / published by arrangement with
Cinergi Productions Inc. and Cinergi Productions N.V.

PRINTING HISTORY
Berkley edition / January 1994

All rights reserved.
Copyright © 1994 by Cinergi Productions Inc.
and Cinergi Productions N.V.
This book may not be reproduced in whole or in part,
by mimeograph or any other means, without permission.
For information address: The Berkley Publishing Group,
200 Madison Avenue, New York, New York 10016.

ISBN 0-425-15806-3

BERKLEY®
Berkley Books are published by
The Berkley Publishing Group, 200 Madison Avenue,
New York, New York 10016.
BERKLEY and the "B" design are trademarks of
Berkley Publishing Corporation.

PRINTED IN THE UNITED STATES OF AMERICA

10 9 8 7 6 5 4 3 2 1

Prologue

In 1879, Geronimo, the last Native American leader to be captured, was still free, leading General Crook and his band of tame Apache scouts on a merry chase through the Arizona Territory, parts of New Mexico, and the rough country of Old Mexico. The land was Geronimo's greatest ally, the hot, baking, dusty, alkali flats, the sudden rearing buttes, the mountains, the relentless sun, the hot wind. The kind of land once described as being hell on women and horses certainly was hell on Crook and his troops and his scouts, because they weren't used to it. It was the kind of land that grew rock, cactus, and sand, and if you couldn't live on those, you couldn't live in that country.

The country had been mostly overlooked by the forty-niners on their way to California to seek gold. But while a lone prospector, a man named Ed Shiefflin, was slowly making his way back east, taking his time, he was intrigued by an ore he had found in the Sierra Madres in Colorado, a lead he followed down into the lower lands to that southeastern part of Arizona.

Friends told him that he was crazy, that the only thing he would find in this godforsaken place was his own death. Instead he found riches beyond his wildest dreams. Riches that brought about not only his death, but the death of many others.

Before the coming of Ed Shiefflin, the country had been sparsely settled by cattlemen who were as much thieves as they were cattlemen. It was nigh on to impossible to scratch out a living in that desolate forbidding territory. What few cattle they managed to keep alive were there solely for the purpose of bearing their registered brands to give legality to the many more head of stolen cattle they brought in from Mexico. They were cattlemen and ranchers only in the sense that they dealt in beef and sold it to people who didn't much care whose beef it was.

But their ranches provided not only a livelihood for them and a place of residence, but a hideout and a safe haven for such outlaws as Curly Bill Brocius, Floren Florentino, and the dangerous Johnny Ringo, men who hid out in the badlands until it was time to make a foray against an unsuspecting traveler, a Mexican with too much gold, a defenseless sodbuster, or an unwary miner. Rough country breeds rough men, and these men were as rough as the country. They were armed to the teeth—not only armed physically, they were also armed mentally. These men dealt in cattle as well as in death.

There was no recreation in that country—no women, no gambling, no whiskey, only what they could import from the little town of Brisbee, thirty miles to the southeast, or what they could find on their raids into Mexico to the south.

The nearest big town was Tucson, a hard three day's ride to the northwest. They didn't get up that way much because they were not welcome, such as they were not welcome in many places. As a consequence, they found their fun in cruelty, in rape, in torment, and in blood. Their mischief was the misery of others.

To their delight and amazement, they saw the town of Tombstone suddenly rising out of the dusty, alkali flats, surrounded by the low hard capped mountains and buttes.

By rights, they should have called it Silver City, after the precious metal that carved its founding. By the time they got around to creating and naming the town, there was already a large graveyard at the end of Freemont Street. There were as many horizontal souls there as there were vertical souls in the town. There was no good reason to name it Tombstone. There were no tombs there, certainly no stone markers to indicate the shallow graves where the men lay with the several unnatural holes that they had acquired in disputes over women, whiskey, or money.

But Tombstone they named her. Queen of the boomtowns. She sprang up overnight, drawing like a magnet the good and the bad, the evil and the simple, the naive and the devious, the lusters and the lusted after, the quick and those not so quick, who really gave the town its name. Not all of them were bad. There were honest miners, honest workers, honest shopkeepers, a few frustrated preachers and schoolteachers. It was said there was even an occasional honest lawyer. But by and large, they were adventurers. They were thieves, bandits, cutthroats, cardsharps, and sharpers of every size, shape, and gender. There were whores, saloonkeepers, madams, purveyors of disease, preyers upon the unwary, and not the least of these, the duly appointed lawmakers. There were lawmen there. Supposedly, men that had been imported by the frantic townspeople to protect themselves from each other. There was the sheriff, such as he was, and he had deputies, such as they were, but it was a little hard to tell which side of the law anyone was on.

The real law was the men who had been there originally and now had banded together as they never had before. They brought in new recruits, they brought in every gun hand, every ruffian, every bandit from that part of the country and formed an organization. To identify themselves, they wore red sashes around their waists—it was their badge of honor, and they called themselves the cowboys and they were the law.

It was fitting, some said, that their sashes were red because that was the major color they dealt in. Their leader was Curly Bill Brocius.

Chapter One

They came racing their horses from across the border, the dust and dirt flying from beneath their horses' hooves. They were dirty, unshaven, greasy, but as they rode, the speed of the horses threw the red sashes back from a string around their waists.

Their leader was Curly Bill Brocius. Besides him to his left rode Johnny Ringo; to his right rode Ike Clanton. To the side of Ike was his younger brother, Billy. Even at that pace, they were laughing and joking as the village of Zacaticus drew nearer and nearer just over the rise in the plain.

Already they could see the young people, the children. They could hear the church bell pealing. They could see the decorations strung around for the wedding.

Curly Bill yelled to his right to Ike Clanton. He said, "Well, looks like they been expectin' us. Looks kinda like they saved some party for us. Reckon there ought to be enough tequila and women to go around."

Curly Bill was a short, stocky man with a grizzled beard and dirty-blondish hair. He wore a pair of denims, inset with leather, worn thin by hours in the saddle. With his patched leather jacket, he wore his narrow-brimmed flat-crowned gray Stetson, both of which were stained with sweat and dust.

There was a rifle in the boot of his saddle and a six-shot revolver at his side. In his waistband, there was Lightning .38. His eyes were mean and pinched looking. When he laughed toward Ike, his teeth were yellow and broken. There was no humor in his laugh.

Ike Clanton grinned back at him. "Well now," he said, "I don't reckon I much care if they are expecting us or not. I figure we'll just make ourselves to home anyhow."

The Clantons had been in southeastern Arizona Territory for the better part of twenty-five years. Their father had died the year before, and Billy and Ike had taken over the running of the ranch. As far as Ike Clanton was concerned, any other settlers were newcomers. It was his steady resolve that the land belonged to the Clantons with maybe some of it due the McClaury's and the McMasters. Ike was known as a loudmouth, but he was also known as a dangerous man, sparing nothing, especially when he had the upper hand. But his brother Billy was the more dangerous of the two. It had been said that Ike talked and sometimes shot.

Billy never did much talking. Both of the brothers had been stealing cattle and killing Mexicans for as long as they could remember.

With the wind at his face, Curly Bill yelled something at Johnny Ringo, but the words were lost in the thunder of their horses' hooves. Ringo just glanced at him. Of the ten men, he was the most mysterious, the most dangerous. He had a thin, almost aesthetic-looking face, but it was the eyes that you noticed first. They were flat. At first glance, there appeared to be nothing there. He just looked at you. He looked at you, and yet you felt something unnerving. It was said that he was an educated man who had somehow gone wrong. Most men stayed clear of him. It was said that he was like a rattlesnake, but that was wrong; a rattlesnake would give you warning. Johnny Ringo never did.

With the exception of Ringo, most of the men were in various degrees of drunkenness. They looked upon the raid of the village as a diversion, a recreation, something that was going to be fun and profitable. But it was also going to be revenge. Of late, the Rurales had been giving them more trouble than they cared for. Most of them were young, in their mid to late twenties. Only Curly Bill Brocius was somewhere in his thirties. No one really knew how old Johnny Ringo was and no one was about to ask.

As they neared the village Curly Bill raised his hand and began to slow his own horse, and the others began to follow suit. A half mile out from Zacaticus, they had slowed their horses down to a trot and then, as they got closer, down to a walk.

They were no longer riding abreast. Now they were strung out in a rough column behind Johnny Ringo and Curly Bill and Ike Clanton. A few of the men were already drawing out their rifles from their saddle boots. A few of them were laughing. Curly Bill spit tobacco juice and looked back.

Chapter Two

It was early afternoon in the little village of Zacaticus and the tiny town was fairly athrob with excitement. Though only ten miles from the Arizona border, the village was poor, full of peons who barely made a living raising corn, scrawny cattle, pigs, and goats.

But today was to be different. Today was to be special. Today was to be a happy day. There was to be a wedding. It would be a cause to celebrate, a chance to forget their poverty and the hard lives that they had led the rest of the year.

One of the sons of the village had risen to the rank of captain of the Mexican Rurales. The Rurale police were known for their valor and daring.

Today he was to wed the prettiest girl in the village. A feast had been prepared. It would be a fiesta. The church had been decorated, all the townspeople would be in their best clothes. There was much gaiety and excitement, for fiestas and feasts were few and far between.

Even the young priest was excited. It would be the first

wedding that he would perform. The bride and groom were standing before him at the altar of the church. The pews were full; outside, the tables were laden for the fiesta. The town was full of excitement as children and the town's young people ran back and forth, waiting for the bride and groom and the wedding party to emerge from the church. It was only moments away.

The bride in her traditional wedding gown was radiant. The groom stood proudly in the uniform of the Rurales, his fellow officers all around him. The favored men and women of the village were in attendance in the church. The place hushed. The priest began the wedding ceremony.

It was not just the fact that there was a wedding that made this day special—no, it was because the young captain of the Rurales was getting married. For he was the leader of the rural police that had fought such a desperate and ceaseless battle against the bandits and the cattle thieves who preyed upon the poor peons. The cattle thieves who came from across the border from Arizona.

When they were within a hundred yards of the first of the adobe homes, Curly Bill pulled the group to a halt and the men dismounted. They left one man behind to hold the horses. The other nine started forward.

As they walked Curly Bill said, "Florentino, get your ass up here. You know I don't speak Mex, ain't ever gonna speak any, so get your ass up here and earn your keep by doin' some of that there interpretin'."

A slim dark man with a scar on his cheek moved forward. Florentino was a half-breed who had just drifted into the group some six months previous. He was no better or no worse than the others. Certainly, he felt no compunction about turning on his own people.

As they reached the first line of adobe shacks, Curly Bill said, not particularly speaking to anyone, "Well, I reckon we'll learn them sons of bitches who to screw with and who not to screw with." He was talking more to himself than to anyone else. "I never cared for nobody messin' around in my business and I figure comin' into Mexico and stealing their sorry-assed cattle is my business. I reckon them cute little boys in their uniforms need to learn it the hard way."

Ike Clanton said, "Yeah."

Billy said, "Why don't we string a few of 'em up?"

Curly Bill just glanced at him. "What do you wanna waste good rope for?"

Johnny Ringo said, "You boys talk a lot, don't ya?" Curly Bill glanced at him but didn't say anything.

They were starting to enter the square now, and as they walked on the hard-packed dirt their long shanked spurs made a *ching, ching, ching* with every step. Around them, the children and the women began to take notice. They froze as they watched these hard men walk toward the plaza, toward the church, toward where the wedding party was soon to emerge.

Ten yards from the doors of the church, Curly Bill raised his hand and stopped. The rest of the men shuffled for a few more steps and halted in a line with their leader.

Johnny Ringo had very deliberately taken himself to the left end of the line, leaned against the table, and crossed his arms.

Under the stares of the frightened onlookers, Curly Bill nonchalantly walked over to a table, picked up a tortilla filled with meat in his left hand, and began to eat. With his right hand, he took up a bottle of tequila, alternating bites of food with slugs of tequila.

From behind him, one of the men said, "Okay we grub down Cruly?"

Without taking his eyes from the front of the church, Curly Bill said, "No."

Just then, the bells of the church began to ring joyously, and moments later the doors were flung open and the happy bride and groom came into the sunlight, followed by the priest and the rest of the wedding party.

After the cool darkness of the church, it took the young captain's eyes a few seconds to adjust. He was almost at the bottom of the church steps before he became aware of the strangers standing before them.

For a second he was confused, then he said tensely in Spanish, "Who are you men and what do you want here?"

Curly Bill glanced sideways at Florentino.

Florentino said, "He say he don' want us here." Curly Bill laughed and looked back at the captain and took another bite of the tortilla. By now, all the men had shifted to their positions; Ike Clanton to his right and Johnny Ringo at the end of the line.

Curly Bill smiled without humor and gestured at the bride and said, "Well, Captain, reckon you want me to break her in for ya?"

The captain stared at him, puzzled for a moment, and then said something to one of his men. After hearing the reply, his face went suddenly white. He glanced quickly to his left and then to his right. The Rurales were unarmed, their rifles stacked neatly near the front door of the church. One of them made a dash toward the rifles, and when he did, one of the cowboys drew and fired at him, shooting him in the back. It was a signal for them all to fire. In unison, some with revolvers and some with rifles, they began to shoot into the crowd of men and even into the women at the edge of the crowd. The townspeople were falling right and left. Johnny Ringo, at the end of the line, watched, amused, taking no hand in the slaughter.

It was over in seconds. At least twelve of the Rurales lay dead or dying on the ground. A few of the young women were spotted with blood on their white dresses.

Only the captain and his bride stood unharmed, the priest, his face white, behind them.

Calmly reloading his revolver, Curly Bill said, "Messican po-lice, huh? Yall ain't nothing. Best part of yall ran down your mamas' legs."

He took two steps and the captain moved in front of his bride. Curly Bill said, "Now you just get down on your knees there, Mr. Rurale Captain."

The captain stared at him. His face was white, but his eyes were open and full of hate. He did not understand what Curly Bill had said.

Curly Bill turned his head and said to Florentino, "Tell that son of a bitch to get down on his knees."

In rapid Spanish, Florentino spoke to the captain. For an answer, the captain spit on the ground, his eyes steely and defiant.

Florentino said to Curly Bill, "He will not kneel. He is proud."

Curly Bill stared and laughed for just a moment, still without humor, then said, "No, this here jus' won't work. Somebody here get this here stick down on his knees."

At his side, Billy Clanton, leveling his double-barrel shotgun, suddenly fired, blowing away the proud captain's shins and dropping him to his knees.

With heavy sarcasm, Curly Bill said, *"Gracias, mi amigo."*

Then he took a few steps, bringing him above the fallen Rurale captain, who was slumped on the ground.

Curly Bill said, "Now, they call me Curly Bill, the founder of the Feast. Now, maybe you don't remember, but me and my boys skylark through your dingy crummy little country just about anytime we damn well please, and big-hat crummy-looking greasers getting in our way ain't allowed. Now, I done warned you once, but I guess you don't hear so good. Now, the warning is all over with. Fact of the matter, your men is all over with, ain't nobody left but you."

He laughed that same unfunny laugh.

At his feet, the captain said something through gasps of pain, something in Spanish.

Florentino smiled. Curly Bill said, "What the hell did he say, you half-breed idiot?"

"He said, what are you waiting for, he know you killing him."

"Well now, how did he figure that out?" Behind the captain, the pale-faced priest spoke haltingly in Spanish. Curly Bill looked at Florentino, who said, "Someone will revenge for them. A sick horse."

Curly Bill said, "A sick horse? What the hell is he talkin' about?"

Ringo came walking lazily from the end of the line. He had not fired a shot. He had not taken part in this slaughter. He said, "That is not what he said, you ignorant wretch. Your Spanish is worse than your English."

From the ground, the captain said in English, *"You . . . go . . . to . . . hell."* The words came out haltingly, each one being forced from his mouth.

Curly Bill just grinned at him and slowly snapped the cylinder on his revolver; he cocked it, aiming it at the captain's head, and said, "You first." Then he fired, shooting the captain in the head.

The force of the bullet knocked the captain back against the legs of his bride, who screamed and fell over her dead husband. Behind them, the priest, his eyes raised toward the heavens, screamed, "Animals! Butchers!"

Ringo stepped forward and drew. With almost no motion, his pistol was in his hand and pointed toward the priest. His pistol seemed to fire of its own volition. One second the priest was standing there, and the next, the force of the bullet had knocked him back onto the steps of the church.

Even as the echo of the shots were sounding throughout the square, a sudden silence fell over the cowboys. They turned slowly to stare at Ringo. He had shot a priest. For a moment the silence held, and then Curly Bill started to laugh. A big Curly Bill laugh.

He looked up at Ringo and said, "What is all that blabber about a sick horse? Somethin' about a sick horse gonna get revenge? That don' make no sense. What's the greaser dog collar talking about?"

With disinterest, Ringo said, "He was just quoting the Bible. Revelation: 'Behold a pale horse and the one that sat on him was Death and Hell followed with him.'"

He smiled thinly at Curly Bill. For a second the words seemed to unsettle the bandit leader, but then he raised his pistol and fired into the air.

The shot sounded unusually loud in the silent square.

He lowered his pistol and grinned at the women, who were frozen in terror around the dead and dying bodies of the Rurales.

He said, "Well, boys, looks like we're gonna have us a fiesta. Let's everybody grab us one of these here gals and have us a dance."

15

One of the cowboys said, "Hell, Curly Bill, how can we have a dance and we ain't got no music?"

Curly Bill grinned at him and said, "Boy, the kind of dancin' I'm talkin' about, you don' need no music."

He holstered up his gun and let out a whoop and started toward the women.

Chapter Three

There was a crowd on the passengers platform of the Tucson depot. The afternoon southbound had just pulled in with its mixture of passenger cars and freight cars. People hurried to board the train and others to depart it and be on their way. Down the train, away from the platform, a tall spare man in a black frock coat and a black flat-brimmed hat was leading a horse down the ramp from a stockcar. To a trained eye, the animal appeared to be a quarter horse bred back to a Morgan. Whatever his breed, he had obviously been well cared for, as shown by his bristling black coat and the way the muscles rippled beneath his skin. The noise of the train station and the ride he had taken on the train down from the north had left the animal nervous, so as they reached the foot of the ramp and the horse once more stood on solid ground, the man took a moment to pet him down and to gentle him.

The man was strong-featured and fair-haired, with a distant look in his gray eyes. He unconsciously glanced in every direction as he gentled the horse, constantly talking to him.

Up the platform at the telegraph office, Crawley Dake, a middle-aged U.S. marshal, was talking to a railway employee when his deputy tapped him on the shoulder and pointed down the track at the man and the horse. Crawley said, "Is that him?"

The man who had tapped him nodded. "I reckon, Marshal Dake. Looks like him. Last time, I seen him in Dodge."

The marshal said, "Why don't you fetch him up here?"

The man who tapped him said, "I reckon not, Marshal. He ain't the kind you just send for. I don't reckon he does much fetchin'."

Dake said, "Hell, I reckon I'll just go down and talk to him if he is that high-and-mighty."

The man said, "Oh, he ain't high-and-mighty at all. Just depends on how you approach him. Know what I mean?"

The marshal walked down the platform and descended the steps and took a few strides toward the man, who was now cinching up the girth of the saddle of the black horse. He had his back to the marshal. The marshal tapped him on the shoulder. The man in the black frock coat didn't bother to look around, just kept on tightening the girth. He said, "Yeah."

"Mr. Earp, my name is Dake, Crawley Dake. I am the U.S. marshal—"

He never got to finish. Wyatt Earp said, "Forget it."

"Excuse me?"

Wyatt Earp finally looked around. He looked at the marshal with flat gray eyes. He said, "I said, forget it. I don't want the job and that's final."

Dake said, "But wait, you don't understand."

"No, Marshal, you don't understand. I did my duty. Now I want to get on with my life. I am going to Tombstone."

For a moment Dake just looked at him. "Off to strike it rich, huh? All right, fine. Wish you luck, but I'll tell you this, though, never was a rich man yet that didn't wind up with a guilty conscience."

For a second a small smile played around Wyatt's lips. He said slowly, "I already got a guilty conscience. Might as well have the money too. Well, good day to you, I gotta get moving."

After the marshal had left, Wyatt Earp stood for a moment holding the reins of his horse, looking around at this new Arizona Territory. He was to meet his brothers here. All three were late of Dodge City, where they had been town marshals. There was Virgil, the eldest of the three, and his wife, Allie. Then the youngest, Morgan, and his young wife, Louisa.

Likewise, all three brothers felt that they had served their time in law enforcement, sometimes for wages less than a hundred dollars a month. Now they considered doing their time with the good life. Their time to use their endeavors to make money, their time to live peacefully and happily without the everlasting threat of a bullet in the back or an ambush, or a crazy man with an eye, or any one of the thousand dangers that had to be faced as towns were tamed through the West.

Standing there, it was difficult to tell how old a man Wyatt was. With his face at rest, he looked comparatively young, almost like he could have been in his late twenties. But there was something about his face, in his eyes especially, that made you think he was older. Perhaps it was because he had done enough living in a short period of time to have lived beyond his years.

Now he stood there staring toward the town, looking for his common-law wife, Celia Ann, whom he called Mattie. For the last two hours on the train, he's watched her fidget and sweat like an alcoholic needing a drink, except he knew that whiskey was not her particular brand of poison.

As soon as the train stopped, she had departed and rushed into town for an apothecary or any other kind of store where she could buy a bottle of laudanum, an opium-based, strong painkiller which she claimed she took for headaches.

But Wyatt knew better. Nobody had that many headaches. They had tried to talk about it sometimes, but it didn't seem to do much good. He had begun by loving her as much as he thought a man could love a woman, but as the months had passed, that love had slowly waned, until now, it was very close to something more like pity.

He was not a particularly big man, standing just about five foot ten inches, slimly built, but with powerful shoulders and strong capable hands. At first glance, he didn't appear to be handsome, but then he could laugh and his whole face changed, and you could see the good and the fun that was inside of him that wanted to come out. There had been too many unhappy times, too much danger, too much badness, too much of the sort of things that killed men's souls, and Wyatt Earp had seen too much of it. Now all he wanted was a chance to be left alone. He was aware of his reputation. He wished he didn't have it.

There was no train service to Tombstone, so the plan was for the three brothers to meet in Tucson and then go by wagon, carrying what household goods that had, on to the boomtown. They had no plans beyond arriving in the town, taking whatever opportunity presented itself. For Wyatt, that usually meant gambling, though Wyatt was not really a gambler. He liked the odds on his side, he liked to run the game, taking the house odds. What Virgil and Morgan were going to do, he had no idea. The brothers had always managed to find a way to get by, but it had been a long time since they had done it without guns.

As Wyatt started toward town, leading his horse and looking for Mattie, Marshal Dake hailed him again. Wyatt stopped and looked around at the lawman. He said, "Yeah."

The marshal said, "Mr. Earp, I'll give you this for what it's worth. I see you aren't armed. Arizona Territory ain't exactly a place to go around unarmed, especially if you are Wyatt Earp."

Wyatt smiled lightly. "They don't shoot unarmed men, do they, Marshal, do they?"

Now it was Marshal Dake's turn to smile. He said, "Well, best I can tell you is that they haven't shot any unarmed women lately anyways."

Wyatt laughed slightly and shook his head and started forward with his horse. Just as he reached the outskirts of the town, which was set very close to the railroad station, he suddenly heard his name being called from off to his right. He turned. A voice from the crowd of people on the boardwalk said loudly, "Boy, I'd know that sour face anywhere."

Wyatt turned around and started toward the speaker, smiling. Coming toward him were his brothers, Virgil and Morgan. Behind them a half-loaded wagon sat at the edge of the station. Virgil was showing streaks of gray in his hair and pounds around his middle. But Morgan was still young and slim, almost identical to Wyatt, except almost a size smaller. Likewise, they were both dressed in black frock coats and wearing black flat-crowned hats. Virgil wore a white ruffled shirt with a black string tie.

As they neared each other Wyatt broke into a wide grin,

then he rushed the next two steps, holding out his arms. He said, "Damn, what are you two no-goods doing here? I reckon you kept me waiting for at least a week. Boy. Hey, Virgil, my God, Morgan, how you doing, boys?"

Morgan said, "Well, how do we look?"

Wyatt said, "You look great, both of you. Even if you are ugly."

Behind the men, Virgil's blond wife, Allie, who was small and fierce and Irish, stepped around Morgan and started toward Wyatt. Virgil said, "Wyatt, you remember Allie?"

Allie said, "Good God, well, he better."

Wyatt hugged her. Laughing, he said, "Allie, girl, and my God, here is Louisa. You are so lovely. I'm at your feet, darling, just at your feet." He turned to Morgan. "Guess it's only right. Ma always said you were the prettiest."

Virgil smiled. "Yeah, but she always liked the ugliest one of the litter." He laughed. "Reckon you know who I'm talking about."

Just as the reunion was ending, Waytt's still-handsome blond wife, Mattie, broke through the crowd and hurried toward the group. He could see by the way she was walking and by the expression on her face that she was still in pain.

Mattie said, "Wyatt, I couldn't find a single store that had any laudanum. I—"

Wyatt cut her off. "Mattie, they're already here. Folks, this is Celia Ann, but you can call her Mattie."

Virgil said, holding out his hand, "Mattie, it's a pleasure."

Morgan came forward to take her hand in his and kiss her on the cheek. Wyatt looked at his brothers, welcoming the woman whom they really didn't know. He tried to smile.

Wyatt said, "Boy, I sure been dreaming about this. God, since forever. I kept waiting. It will just be us—us and the good times."

Wyatt glanced behind him, seeing a large plate-glass window in the depot station house. He said, "Yall come on over here. I want to show you something." Then, with his arms outstretched, he herded them toward the window, taking them near enough so that the group was reflected in the plate-glass window. He said, "Look at us." With his arms, he pulled them closer together.

"Just look at us. Look at us. It's like a family portrait, ain't it?"

In his voice and in his demeanor you could almost see and hear the happy man that Wyatt Earp would have been had he not had all the trouble in his past. As they stood there Virgil glanced over at his younger brother. Standing there together, seeing themselves in the family portrait, gave him a sense of unease. It was as if Wyatt knew something or felt something. Like Wyatt knew what this was. This might be the last time that there would ever be such a peaceful feeling.

But he swallowed his misgivings and smiled over at Wyatt and said, "Well, this would be mighty fine if you and Morgan's ugly pusses wasn't in the picture. Now, if yall would just step away and let me and these here pretty ladies pose, that would be just fine for the photographers to come out and take a shot. I mean with a camera." Then he laughed. "That's the only kind of shot I want anymore."

Wyatt looked at him for a second. Finally, he smiled. He said, "Yeah, I know what you mean."

Mattie was turning to him, her face still anxious. She said, "Wyatt, didn't you hear me, I couldn't find any laudanum, honey. Help me, please. We might have to find a doctor."

Morgan's wife, Louisa, said, "Mattie, honey, what's the matter?"

Mattie said, "Oh, I've just got this headache. I need some laudanum."

Wyatt was frowning.

Louisa said, "Honey, I've got just the thing." She began rummaging through her large handbag. "I've got some Lydia Pinkham's Tonic. You know the kind of stuff you take for cramps for that time of month. Helps with headaches too."

Mattie said anxiously, "No, no, no. That's not what I need."

Wyatt said, almost angrily, "Can't you wait? Can't you wait until we say hello properly?"

Just then Allie stepped forward, putting her hand in her purse. She said, "Mattie, not to worry. I've got a little bottle of laudanum right here. You're right, it really will knock out a headache." She took the little bottle of clear liquid and handed it to Wyatt's wife.

Almost frantically, Mattie grabbed for the bottle. She turned and walked a little way away from the group. Wyatt turned his head slightly so that he could see her as she took the bottle and put it to her lips and tipped her head back. He shook his head. His brothers looked at each other, knowing.

Wyatt changed the subject and took the attention away from Mattie. He said, "Hey, Virge, you see Doc Holliday while you were in Prescott?"

Virgil said, "He was hitting the streets when we left, he and Kate."

Allie said, with feline malice, "Oh, that woman."

Wyatt laughed. "I miss Doc. I miss that old rip."

Virgil said, "I don't."

Allie said, "Neither do I."

Wyatt smiled slightly. "Doc makes me laugh. Of all the

men I know, he just don't give a damn. I never met a man who just flat don't give a damn."

Morgan said, "Maybe that's because he don't have nothing to give a damn about."

"Well, he makes a damned good friend, and you can't say that about that many people. When it comes down to it, outside of you two, I would rather have Doc Holliday standing next to me, especially if it's a tight place."

At the back of the saloon, five men were sitting around a table playing poker. Four of them were ordinary-looking gamblers and ruffians, but one stood out, not only because of his dress, but because of his elegant manners and the look about him that immediately drew your attention. He was dressed in a bright linen frock coat and a brocaded vest. It was not his clothes that drew your attention, but the air about him.

At first you thought it was pleasant, but then you saw the menacing, as he moved and waved his hands about, and you caught a glimpse of his ivory-handled .44 just under his coat.

Occasionally, he made a slight rumbling in his throat. The tubercular cough. It was with him constantly.

His name was Doc Holliday and he had come west to die. By profession, he was a dentist. By choice, he was a gambler and a killer. In size, he was small and weighed no more than a hundred and forty pounds.

Near him stood his mistress, Kate Horany. She was an elegant-looking woman, striking rather than beautiful. In spite of the heat, she was wearing a blue velveteen gown and holding a fur muff in her hands.

At the slightest gesture from Doc, she stepped over to the table and poured whiskey into his silver drinking cup. The other men at the table glared at her and glared at Holliday.

One of them, a man named Ed Bailey, said, "Are we gonna play poker or not? It's five hundred, up to you. Are you in or out?"

Doc smiled slightly. "Well, I suppose I'm deranged, but I'll just have to call." He looked up at Kate. He said, "Cover your ears, darling. Liable to be some shouting and some arm waving around here."

With a slight motion of his hand, Holliday threw in five one-hundred-dollar chips.

Doc said, deceptively mildly, "Mr. Bailey, I am surprised at you. Just because I have a daisy of a hand. Well, I reckon I am astounded at your manners, sir."

The anger was red upon Bailey's face. He said, "Just pick up your money and go. I'm sick of listening to you and that smart-aleck voice of yours. In fact, I am sick of you."

"Now, Ed, are we cross?"

"Listen, you skinny lunger," Bailey said, "your guns don't impress me. If it wasn't for your guns, you wouldn't be nothing."

Doc leaned forward, opening his coat as he did, revealing the .45-caliber Colt Peacemaker and the .38-caliber Colt revolver he had stuck in his belt.

Doc said, "You mean these little daisies?"

Bailey's face was flushed with mounting anger. He said, "Why don't you get the hell out of here?" He jerked his head toward Kate. "And take that whore of yours with you."

The whole saloon seemed to go very quiet. The other men unconsciously seem to push their chairs back, but all Doc did was let a little smile play around his face.

With a delicate motion, he plucked both of his revolvers out from underneath his coat and laid them carefully on the table.

He said, "Now, Ed, that wasn't a very nice thing to say." He sat back, seeming to remove himself from the guns. He said, "Would I talk about friends of yours like that?"

Bailey looked uneasy. He realized he had gone too far. He said, "I don't like you, Holliday, or any of your kind, understand me?"

In a disarmingly mild voice, Doc Holliday said, "Why, Ed, what an ugly thing to say. Does that mean that you are not my friend anymore? You know, Ed, if I thought you weren't my friend, I don't think I could bear it."

With a slight nod of his head, he indicated his guns lying on the table. He said, "Now, there are my little daisies growing on the table. Can't we be friends again?"

Bailey glared at him nervously. He was uncertain. He glanced at the other three men at the table. They studiously avoided his eyes.

Doc said, "What about it, Ed, can't we be friends?" He leaned forward slightly. "But remember, Ed, friendship is trust, so please don't hurt me. You are so much bigger than I am."

Doc's smile increased as he stared at Bailey. His right hand had casually fallen down into the pocket of his linen frock coat.

For a second, tension hung heavy in the air, and then Bailey boiled over. He jumped up and lunged at Doc. Almost languidly, Doc was suddenly on his feet; his left arm reached out and grabbed Bailey by the hair and jerked him toward him. Bailey's hands went up toward his head to free Doc's grasp from his hair. As he did Doc's right fist suddenly flew up into Bailey's right armpit.

A shocked look came over Bailey's face.

And then in quick succession, Doc landed three, four, then five more blows under Bailey's armpit. The blows seemed to be too light to be doing any damage, but so fast was the movement of Holliday's hand that it was only as he stopped and rested his hand, his fist on the table, that it could be seen that he was holding a knife with four deadly inches of blade exposed.

Bailey began to sink slowly backward, blood streaming down his left side. Doc released the man's hair. Bailey fell back to the edge of his chair, tried to grab the armrest, and then fell heavily to his side on the floor.

From behind the bar, the bartender reached down and came up with a shotgun. But Kate had casually drifted around toward his direction. As he leveled the shotgun Kate's hand came out of the muff holding a derringer. She put the barrel to the bartender's ear. He froze.

Kate said, "Put that shotgun down, or I'll burn a hole through your head."

Carefully and slowly, the bartender laid the shotgun on the top of the bar and raised his hands.

At the table, Doc Holliday put the knife back in his coat and picked up both of his guns and put them back in his pockets. He stepped back from the table and said, "Now, Kate, my darling, if you will be so kind as to collect our winnings, we'll be on our way."

While Kate came over to the poker table and converted the chips in front of Doc and the pot he just won into cash from the cigar box that was being used as a bank, Doc covered the room with a gun in each hand. He said to Kate as she was counting the money, "Now, Kate, darling, just take what's ours. We wouldn't want to cheat these gentlemen, now, would we?"

As he finished speaking a sudden spasm of deep racking coughs took Doc Holliday. His thin frame shook. Kate looked up at him anxiously.

The coughing went on for almost a minute, but Doc's guns never left the people they were covering. When he finally gasped in a calm breath, one of the gamblers said to him, "Doc, how come you never cough until it's all over with? How come you never cough when things are kinda hot?"

Doc said, "Well, it's the timing of the thing, my friend. Tends to make the hands shake, and we can't have that."

Kate said, "We're ready, Doc."

Still holding his guns, Doc walked around the table to where Bailey was lying on the floor. The man was still alive, but obviously in pain. Doc looked down at him and said, "Does it hurt?"

For an answer, Bailey groaned. He said, "Oh, my God."

Doc said, "Gooood."

With Kate by his side, he started backing toward the door. "Well, gentlemen, I suppose this is good evening, then," Doc said.

The gamblers stared at him, none of them making a move. Bailey lay on the floor, blood staining the wood.

At the door, Doc said, nodding his head toward Bailey, "Gentlemen, I think the Christian thing to do would to be call that man a doctor. Something tells me that he has sustained an injury. We will now bid you adieu."

Outside, Doc said, "I calculate that's the end of this town, and let's not bother about the luggage, darling."

Kate smiled at him and reached up and gave him a peck on the cheek as they moved down the street toward the livery stable.

Chapter Four

They reached Tombstone that morning. They had left the wagon and the women just outside of town while the three of them went into the business district to get the lay of the land. Just before they left, Mattie had taken Wyatt aside and pleaded with him to bring her a bottle of laudanum. He had looked at her, partly in distress and partly in sympathy.

He said, "Mattie, can't you just lean on me?"

She smiled her sick nervous smile, her lips twisted. She said, "Wyatt, have you ever tried to lean up against a wall and found it wasn't there?"

There was nothing that he could answer to that, nothing that he could say. It was all too true. She had failed him, but in many ways, he had also failed her.

He looked at her and said, "Mattie, I am sorry."

"Sorry for what, Wyatt? I didn't think that the Earp brothers were ever sorry for anything they did."

He looked at her. For a second he was silent. Then he said, "Mattie, you might be surprised someday at what goes on inside of me. But right now, all I can tell you is that I am sorry, and I hope one day that I can make it up to you."

"You can start by getting me that laudanum." Her voice quavered from the inner shakes that were racking her.

Wyatt nodded slowly. "I'll stop at the first apothecary shop that I see, and I'll bring it right back to you, Mattie, but will you promise me something?"

"What?"

"Will you try to eat something?"

Her lips twisted again. "Wyatt, you've never had a raging weakness inside you." Her voice broke a little. "You don't know what it feels like to be so weak, so dependent."

There was nothing more he could say. He started up Freemont Street, where his brothers were waiting for him. Virgil looked up and said quietly, "Wyatt, it ain't gonna get no better."

Wyatt said, "Virge, there is just some things that a man don't need no advice on."

"I understand that, Wyatt. But you are still my brother, and I can't stand to see anything hurt you. Do you love her that much?"

"It ain't got nothing to do with love, Virgil. Can't you understand that?"

Morgan said, "We understand that it's eating you alive. We have seen three days of it from Tucson. I hate to see her hurting, but I hate to see your hurting worse."

Wyatt said, "Why don't we just get on about our business and leave this to me. Would that be all right with you fellows?"

For an answer, they turned and started up the street.

As they walked they looked at the booming vitality of the town of Tombstone. It was new, it was colorful. Part town, part mining camp. A wild mixture of brightly painted wooden storefronts with half-finished stone buildings rimmed by clusters of tents and shanties all perched atop a small hill with a view of the desert and the purple-lagoon mountains beyond.

There was a feeling of urgency about the town, as if you should have arrived an hour earlier, or if not an hour earlier, at least a day, or better still, a week, or even better than that, a month before. People hurried by on both sides of them, their pace quickening with every step.

You could hear the vibrant din of hammers and saws, player pianos, hurdy-gurdies, the clip-clopping of horses hooves, and the wild laughter from saloon after saloon after saloon.

The town bustled with drovers, with cowboys, with miners, but Chinamen, and sullen, gun-toting hard cases.

Ahead of them, they could see a commotion in front of a small-town cottage. A wagon was parked there, and as the Earps neared they could see a sobbing woman sitting in the middle of the street while her husband tried to comfort her. Three small children stood beside them, watching in stunned silence, as Frank Stillwell, cocky and arrogant, and Pony Deal, a half-breed Indian, heaved their belongings and furniture into the street while snarling, "Shut up you fuckin' deadbeats and move it!"

The Earps stopped, staring at the scene.

Virgil said, "What the hell is going on?"

Frank Stillwell looked up at him and said, "What the hell do you care?"

Morgan said, "Maybe we care."

The half-breed pulled a gun. He said, "Ain't healthy."

Wyatt pulled at Virgil's arm. "We ain't here for that, Virge. Let's move on."

Virgil gave him a glance, and then led the way up the street.

They walked until they stopped in front of the Grand Hotel. It was a two-story frame structure, newly built, and as much as any other building in town deserved the name "grand."

Virgil said, "We gotta find some place to put the women up. They've been sleeping for three nights in a row out on that prairie, and you know women, they gotta have some place prettied up."

As they stood there a handsome well-dressed man wearing an ornate sheriff's badge and a ready smile came walking toward them.

The sheriff said, "Newcomers, eh? Name is Johnny Behan. I'm the Cochise County sheriff. You just hit town?"

Wyatt said, "Just this minute. I'm Wyatt Earp, and these here are my brothers."

Behan raised his eyebrows slightly. "Wyatt Earp, Dodge City. That Wyatt Earp?"

"We gave all that up. We're going into business."

"Well, I'm the man to see. Besides sheriff, I'm also the tax collector, captain of the fire brigade, and chairman of the Nonpartisan, Anti-Chinese League. Got a place to stay yet?"

"No."

Behan said, "Well, I also sit on the town lot commission, and we have three lovely cottages coming up for rent. Not gonna get anything better."

Virgil slowly looked back toward where the family was still sitting in the street. He said, "Like that one there?"

Behan looked at him. He said, "Business is business."

Virgil said, "Yeah."

Wyatt said quickly, "Sounds good. We'd like to take a

look at them. But for the time being, we are standing in mighty bad need of accommodations." He nodded his head toward the Grand Hotel. "Reckon they'd have three rooms?"

John Behan smiled slowly. He said, "For the Earp brothers? Why, I'd reckon that could be arranged. I reckon they'd be honored to have such illustrious clientele. I reckon it would hold the noise down somewhat."

Morgan said, "Wyatt's done explained we're through with all that."

Behan gave him a wink. "Why sure, of course, I understand. Why don't yall just come on in with me and let's get this matter settled and get on with finding you some permanent housing."

As they started up the steps to the hotel, Behan said, "I can't tell you what a relief it is to have some solid citizens moving in here. You ain't gonna believe what kind of riffraff this town is drawing."

Virgil said, "Yeah."

The next morning, right after breakfast, Morgan was standing on the steps of the hotel with Virgil and Fred White, who was the town marshal. Wyatt was walking down the boardwalk, fresh from the barbershop, when Morgan gave him a hail and said, "Wyatt, come over here and meet an old friend. This is Fred White, the town marshal."

Wyatt said, shaking hands, "Pleased to meet you. Seems to be a lot of law around here. We just met the county sheriff yesterday."

White laughed, "Who, Behan? He ain't no law. The only real law here is the cowboys."

Beside him, Virgil said, "The cowboys, yeah, we've been

hearing about them for a couple days. They supposed to be bad news?"

White said, "Nobody does nothing around here without them. They're it. There's a couple of them right there. You can always spot a cowboy, they always wear those red sashes around their waists."

Wyatt looked over in the direction White indicated and saw two rough-looking men with red sashes draped around their waists.

"They look like they still have the bark on them. Well, so long as they don't bother me, I don't figure to bother them," he said.

White gave him a look. He said, "Sometimes they don't give you no choice."

Still looking at the two men, Wyatt said, "That just might be too bad, then."

The two cowboys were lounging in front of the Crystal Palace Saloon. Wyatt recognized them as the two men who had been evicting the family the afternoon before. As Wyatt watched, Frank McMasters and John Behan came out of the saloon and joined the two men.

Wyatt said, with a slight smile on his face, "Is Sheriff Behan fixin' to make an arrest?"

Fred White said, "Not very damned likely—that is, unless they arrest him."

Morgan said, "Are they as rough as they look?"

Virgil spoke. He said, "Like any other hard cases, you just gotta know how to handle them."

"Well, I'm no Wild Bill," Fred White said. "The way I handle them is just mainly live and let live. Plain fact is," White said, "saloons."

Wyatt said, "What about all these saloons?"

Fred White said, "Ah, well, see, that's the real mother

lode here in Tombstone. Twenty-four hours a day. Liquor, hostesses, gambling, making money hand over fist. All except the Oriental. That's a regular slaughterhouse. That's the one saloon nobody goes in. Certainly not the high rollers. The money men won't go near it. Too bad. It's a nice place, but it's a bad place."

Wyatt looked up and down the street. He said, "The Oriental Saloon? Where is it at?"

White motioned with his chin. "Just up the street about a block on your right. You can't miss it. It's the only place that don't have no customers, or if it does, you'll see one come flying out the door. That will be the first sign."

Wyatt started up the street. He said slowly, "Sounds just about like the kind of place that I'm looking for."

Virgil glanced at him. He said, "I thought we were gonna take this kinda slow. Take our time and look around."

Morgan laughed lightly. He said, "Have you ever noticed what slow is to Wyatt? Yesterday is slow to Wyatt."

Fred White said, "I hear you boys gave up the law business. Is that right?"

Wyatt said, "Yeah, we're all through with that. I'm looking for honest work."

Morgan said, "Like dealing faro?"

Wyatt smiled slightly. He said, "Well, work is work. I'll deal faro or I'll milk cows or I'll play the fiddle. Whichever one I'm best at."

Morgan said, "Now, I wonder which one that will be?"

The Oriental Saloon was big enough to hold at least two hundred assorted gamblers and drinkers and hostesses and bartenders. But as Wyatt Earp came through the batwing doors and stopped to survey the place, it was as empty as a new barn.

The player piano was playing the song of the day, "The Lily and the Rose," and behind the bar was the sole bartender, Milt Joyce, the owner. The roulette table was empty, the bar was empty, and the dice tables were empty. Only at the faro table were three players bucking the tiger against the dealer.

As Wyatt Earp stood there, adjusting his eyes to the new cool darkness of the place, Milt Joyce busily started wiping the bar. He said, "Yes, sir, yes, sir. What's your pleasure mister—whiskey, women, or a game of chance?"

Wyatt Earp slowly walked over to the bar, glancing at the faro game at the back. He put one foot on the brass railing, leaned an elbow on top of the bar, and said to Joyce, "Let me have one of those." He pointed to a box of cigars.

Joyce handed him a cigar, and Earp flipped a quarter on the bartop. As if deep in thought, he took his time with the business of cutting off the tip of the cigar and carefully rolled it between his fingers and then finally put it in his mouth, where he lit it. When he got it drawing good, he took another slow look around the saloon. He said, "Kinda nice in here. You run it?"

The bartender put out his hand, which Earp took and shook, and said, "Milt Joyce, owner and operator, such as it is."

"Wyatt Earp."

Joyce laughed and said, "Yeah, and I'm Judge Roy Bean and this here is the Dirty Lily Saloon."

Wyatt took no notice of the sarcasm. He'd heard it before. "Well, excuse me for asking, Milt, but ain't it kinda dead in here? Looks to me like a place like this should be doing a pretty good business. At least the rest of the saloons around town are. Ain't you selling what they're buying?"

Joyce pointed toward the faro table. "See that bird over

there, the dealer?" He was pointing at Johnny Tyler, an unshaven, pug-ugly with a big .45 carried openly in a shoulder holster. As they watched he dealt to a couple scruffy-looking drifters. One of them advanced a stack of chips toward one of the cards. Tyler instantly reacted.

Tyler said, his voice hard, "You back that queen again, you son of a bitch, and I'll blow you right out of the chair. This here is a fair game. Fair is what I say is fair. You understand that, you backcountry jake-legged son of a bitch?"

Back at the bar, Wyatt glanced at Joyce, surprised that he did nothing to interfere with the dealer and the customer. Joyce just shrugged. He said, "He scares off all the high-class play. All that comes in here now is bummers and a few drovers and the occasional drummer from out of town. Just the dregs. Just the ones that don't have enough money to worry about losin'."

Wyatt said mildly, "Why don't you get rid of him and get a straight dealer?"

"Well sure, stranger, that's easy for you to say. My mistake was letting Johnny Tyler in here to begin with. Now I'm afraid it's a little too late," Joyce said.

Wyatt looked interested. He said, "If he was out of here, would you have room for a faro dealer?"

Joyce eyed him. "Yeah, I can always use a good faro dealer. You happen to be one? And there is still the problem of Johnny Tyler."

Wyatt said, "Oh, I don't think he is so much of a problem. What cut do your faro dealers take?"

Joyce scratched his head. "Well, normally I'd pay about fifteen percent, but to get rid of Johnny Tyler, I reckon I'd give the right man a quarter interest in all the games."

Wyatt looked at him. "Yeah?"

"Yeah."

Wyatt carefully laid his cigar in the ashtray. Then, sort of squaring his shoulders, he walked slowly toward the faro dealer, his spurs *ching-ching*ing on the hard floor. Behind him, Milt Joyce came around from the bar and was standing just a few feet behind Wyatt, watching with interest.

For a few moments Tyler didn't react, just went on with the game. And then he became aware of Wyatt Earp's eyes fastened on him. He glanced up. He said, a snarl in his voice, "Somethin' on your mind, stranger?"

Wyatt said, "Well, I just wanted to politely let you know that you are sitting in my chair. If you don't mind getting out, I'd be much obliged."

Tyler stared at him, half-amused. "That's a fact?"

Wyatt said, laughing, "That's a fact." For a long few seconds Tyler looked Wyatt over, running his eyes from Wyatt's boots up to his hat. A small, sneering smile appeared on his face. He said, "For a man that ain't packin', you run your mouth kinda reckless. You trying to get yourself hurt, fella?"

Wyatt said softly, "I don't need to carry a gun to get the edge on a dude like you."

Tyler eyed him again. He picked up a cigar and put it in his mouth. The smoke rolled in a lazy blue haze above his head. He said, "That a fact?"

"It's a fact."

Tyler said sarcastically, "Well, I'm just real scared. I don't reckon I'll be able to take a piss for a good long while, I'm so scared."

Wyatt said quietly, "Damn right you're scared. I can see it in your eyes."

The words seemed to fall one by one like heavy weights

from his lips, each one of them hitting Johnny Tyler like a bullet.

Wyatt suddenly took a step forward. His eyes had gone black and hard. Tyler could sense that something had changed. Almost reflexively, his hand began to move toward his gun. The other players at the table began to back away. Wyatt nodded, his voice calm and steady.

Wyatt said, "Go ahead, skin it out. Skin out that smoke wagon and see what happens."

"Listen, mister, I'm getting tired—"

The words were suddenly cut off as Wyatt slapped him in the face, making his teeth clack together. It was a hard slap, a demeaning slap, a hurtful slap, a shaming slap.

Wyatt said, "I'm getting tired of your gas. Jerk that pistol out and go to work, dammit."

Tyler had gone pale, all pretense of courage gone now. Wyatt slapped him again.

Wyatt said, his voice flat. "I said throw down, boy, I said pull out that cigar and smoke it, I said get to work, boy, can't you hear?"

He slapped Tyler again, harder this time, a backhanded slap. Tyler sat in his chair, frozen. Blood dripped down his chin.

Wyatt said, his voice hard, "Are you going to do something, dammit, or are you just gonna stand there and bleed? What are you, some kind of sissy?"

It was clear that Tyler was done, finished. He sat there and slowly began to tremble. Without saying a word, Wyatt reached over his shoulder, and removed Tyler's weapon from his waistband. He handed the gun to Milt Joyce.

He said, "I reckon this one is finished here, Milt. Ain't you, Johnny?"

Tyler just stared up at him, his hands grasping the back

rail of the chair, his knuckles white, his whole body trembling.

Wyatt said as Milt Joyce took the gun, "Here's a keepsake for you, Milt. Is the job mine?"

Milt Joyce said, his voice unsteady, "I would reckon."

Wyatt turned his attention back to Johnny Tyler. He said, "All right, youngster, out you go." He leaned forward and took Tyler by the ear, lifting him out of the chair and dragging him across the room like an unruly child. At the door, he gave the ear a final twist. Tyler let out a yell. Wyatt assisted him out the door, holding his ear and giving him a boot to the rump. As Tyler went through the batwing doors Wyatt called after him, "And don't come back. Ever. Not if you like the way you look."

Wyatt turned back to where Milt Joyce was standing with his mouth open. He said, "I thought you said that man was tough. That was pretty easy."

Milt Joyce just looked at him, his mouth half-open. He said, almost in a whisper, "My God, you are Wyatt Earp."

Later that afternoon, Wyatt walked into the lobby of the Grand Hotel. His brothers, Virgil and Morgan, were standing near a pillar, smoking cigars. Wyatt walked up to them. He said, "Well, we're off and running. I just acquired us a quarter interest in the Oriental."

Virgil just smiled knowingly. "Acquired?"

Wyatt answered him. "Well . . . so to speak."

Morgan said, "You are the one, Wyatt. You beat anything I've ever seen." But down the block, unseen by the Earps, a wild-eyed Johnny Tyler was advancing on the Grand Hotel with a sawed-off shotgun. He had followed Wyatt Earp to the hotel and then run for his shotgun. Now he was tracking the former marshal of Dodge City. He took up a position on the sidewalk, no more than twenty feet from the front door.

Virgil said, "Why don't we take a walk around town and see what's stirring?"

Wyatt said, "Where are the girls?"

Morgan said, "Oh, they are doing women stuff. Getting the houses ready. You know what women are like. Right now, I reckon they've got a broom in one hand and a dustpan in the other. The next thing you know, we'll all be buying furniture. That faro game of yours had better pay off."

They had reached the door and stepped out onto the sidewalk. Even though they all looked around, not one of them had noticed Johnny Tyler with his shotgun.

They were about to move off when a voice to Wyatt's left called out, "Why, Johnny Tyler, you madcap, where are you going with that shotgun?"

The Earps' heads snapped around at the sound of the voice. They saw Johnny Tyler, frozen, his hand clutching his shotgun. Then they saw Doc Holliday, standing in his doorway, smiling.

Johnny Tyler said, his voice trembling, "Doc, I didn't know you were in town."

The brothers started toward Doc. As they came up only Wyatt put his hand out and shook Doc's hand. He never so much as glanced at Johnny Tyler. Though it was not said, or even indicated, you could sense a strong bond between Wyatt and Doc Holliday.

Wyatt said, "Doc, how the hell are you?"

Doc said, "Perfect, Wyatt, simply perfect." He nodded his head at Johnny Tyler. "Though I must say, you are still up to your old ways. Wyatt, you attract such undesirables as this young scalawag here. What do you aim to do with that shotgun, Johnny Tyler?"

Tyler stared at Wyatt Earp, the shotgun slowly easing down toward his side. He said, "Wyatt? Wyatt Earp?"

Morgan was ignoring Johnny Tyler. He said to Doc Holliday, "We're going into business for ourselves. Wyatt just got a faro game."

Doc smiled. "Since when is faro a business?"

Wyatt said, "Didn't you always say that gambling was an honest trade?"

"I said poker is an honest game. Only a sucker bucks the tiger. The odds are all with the house. Of course, you wouldn't have it any other way, now, would you?" He winked. "Just like in a gunfight."

Wyatt laughed. "Depends on how you look at it. I mean, it's not like anybody's holding a gun to their heads."

"That's what I love about Wyatt. He can talk himself into anything."

Still frozen near the door, Tyler tried to bring his nerves under control. Finally, Doc Holliday glanced around at him and said, "Oh, sorry, Johnny. I forgot all about you. You can run along now."

Wyatt looked at him with a smirk. "Just leave the shotgun."

Tyler leaned the shotgun against the side of the building. He started backing away and said, "Thank you."

Wyatt reached out and picked up the shotgun as Tyler hurried off. For a second he looked it over, then, almost casually, he handed it over to Doc Holliday. "Here, Doc, here's a present for you. You may need it someday, the kind of shot you are." Doc Holliday laughed.

As they were talking Sheriff Behan came walking by. Wyatt said, "Sheriff, this is Doc Holliday."

Doc just looked at the sheriff. "Forgive me if I don't shake hands."

Behan said, "Well, how does our little town suit you?"

Wyatt said, glancing at Doc Holliday, "Fine, just fine."

"Well, it won't be long until our little town will be as big as San Francisco."

The words were no more than out of his mouth when a bullet whizzed past Behan's head and thudded into the wall of a nearby building.

Doc said, "And just as sophisticated."

Suddenly there was more gunfire as a man holding his bloody throat reeled out the door of the nearby Crystal Palace, his gun firing wildly like a sputtering engine before he pitched face-first onto the sidewalk, dead. Immediately two more men appeared: one a staggering drunk with a bullet hole in his shoulder, and Turkey Creek Jack Johnson, a leathery plainsman with his gun at the ready. A crowd formed as the drunk raised his pistol, bellowing.

"You son of a bitch."

Johnson just stood there, coolly. He said, "That's right, keep comin', keep comin'. . . ."

Doc said to Behan, "Very cosmopolitan, Sheriff, very cosmopolitan."

Sheriff Behan hurried toward the two men. Lifting his voice, Wyatt said, "Sheriff, I know that man. That's Creek Johnson. You'd best let him settle his own differences."

Suddenly a third man appeared. This was Texas Jack Vermillion, a long-haired, hawk-nosed, mean-faced man. He held his pistol out and ready, keeping the bystanders at bay.

Vermillion said, including the sheriff in his words, "Easy, gents. This here is a private affair."

But as he finished speaking he spotted Wyatt Earp.

Without taking his fingers out of the action, he said, "Wyatt. Hey, Doc. How yall doin'?"

The drunk said, "You bastards."

The drunk had now raised his gun to where it was almost level. Turkey Creek Johnson said, "Yeah, good. Right about that." Then he fired. The bullets took the drunk dead in the chest, knocking him backward into a heap. For a second Turkey Creek Johnson watched the man he had just killed to make certain that he did not move.

Then he turned and said, "Did I hear somebody mention Wyatt Earp and Doc Holliday?"

Wyatt called, "Over here, Turkey."

Johnson said, "Hello, Wyatt. Hiya, Doc."

Wyatt said, "What was all that about?"

Turkey Creek just shook his head. "Aw, just drunks. Welshed on a bet. Called me a liar. But hell, you can't shoot a man but once—at least not if you do it right."

Doc, with a sort of malicious satisfaction, turned to Sheriff Behan and said, "Sheriff, may I present a pair of fellow sophisticates, Turkey Creek Jack Johnson and Texas Jack Vermillion? Watch your ear, Creek."

They were just discussing the fact that a lucky shot by the drunk had knicked Jack Johnson's ear when the town marshal, Fred White, arrived.

"Gentlemen, I'm afraid I'll have those guns."

"It was a fair fight. We were legal."

White said, "I'm sorry, boys, but I've gotta take you before Judge Spicer."

Johnson looked at Jack Vermillion and said, "Well, law and order, every time, that's us." They handed over their guns while Virgil looked over the two dead men lying in the street and said, "Hell, what kind of town is this?"

The stagecoach had suddenly pulled in right at the end of

the gunfight. It was now beginning to discharge its passengers. The first person out was a woman, striking in her dark, sophisticated, mysterious beauty. They all stared at her.

Jack Vermillion said, "Nice scenery."

She was Josephine Marcus, an actress and singer. For just a moment she stood there, staring boldly back at the men who stood just a few feet from her.

It seemed as if her eyes and the eyes of Wyatt Earp's locked instantly together. Some sort of impression, some sort of magnetism seemed to pass between them. She had an exotic look about her. A look that took her out of the ordinary of any woman that Wyatt Earp could ever remember seeing.

Sheriff Behan's voice was a jarring distraction when he said, "That must be the theatrical troupe. There is a show tonight at Shiefflin Hall."

Wyatt Earp and Josephine Marcus continued to stare at each other, even as another actor and actress stepped out from the coach and stood beside her.

"Yeah, we got tickets."

Turkey Johnson said, "Wyatt, are you going to the show? We'll see you there." He turned to Fred White and said, "Won't we?"

White said, "Yeah, probably. Right now, let's get on over to see the judge and get this here matter settled."

Wyatt and Josephine continued to hold each other's eyes.

Of the people there, only Doc Holliday seemed to be aware of what was going on. He smiled a slow smile and said in a bemused, cynical voice, "Well, well, well. What an enchanted moment."

Wyatt slowly broke his eyes away from Josephine and gave Doc a look and said, "And what is that supposed to mean?"

From down the street, Frank Stillwell and the half-breed Pony Deal watched as the actors exited the coach for the hotel. Josephine led the way, chatting with the handsome lead actor, a man known simply as Fabian.

Josephine said, her voice light and lifting, "Interesting little scene. I wonder who that tall man was?"

Almost imperceptibly she nodded her head toward Wyatt Earp. Fabian let his graceful, aloof gaze swing toward where the brothers were standing. He said, in his actor's voice, "Typical frontier type. Long and lean. And those gray eyes. Like a wild hawk. You see quite a few of his type out here."

Josephine shivered slightly. "Oh, I want one."

Fabian gave her a glance. He said, "Perhaps I do too."

Josephine laughed.

They had started toward the door, but their way was blocked by a large man in an Eastern business suit. They had to pull back because he had almost shoved the door into Josephine's face. With a few strides, Sherman McMasters tipped his hat and followed her and the company of actors into the hotel. For a moment the door remained closed. Then it suddenly flew open and the man in the Eastern business suit came sailing out, followed by McMasters, who held him long enough to give him one final kick. Then McMasters dusted his hands off, turned, and went back inside the hotel.

Chapter Five

The Birdcage Theater, like most of the buildings in Tombstone, was not quite finished, but the crowd who filled it to the rafters could have cared less.

There was plenty of money in the town but little to spend it on except for whores and whiskey and crooked card games. Even the members of the lowest rung of society were determined to get their fair share of culture, as represented by the traveling theater groups.

The show had not started yet and the houselights were still up. The audience was raucous, loud, and near pandemonium.

Curly Bill, Ringo, and their cowboy entourage formed a block in the center rows. Billy Breakenridge, Sheriff Behan's bespectacled, slightly effeminate little deputy, made his way up and down the aisles, timidly, amid the occasional fistfights and yelling matches. A cocky young cowboy called out to him, "Hey, sister boy. Gimme some."

Curly Bill said, "Hey, shut up, Barnes." He motioned to Breakenridge. "Here, sit here, Billy."

Happy as a lark, Breakenridge took his seat next to Curly Bill.

Up above, the Earps were sitting in a box. The women were thrilled to be out for a night on the town.

Allie said, "This is so much fun. We haven't been to a show in years. Isn't it grand to get all dressed up and see such sights?"

Mattie said, "I hope they are good." Her face looked pasty and her hands were shaky.

Just at that moment Doc entered the box, with Kate by his side. At the sight of the woman, the Earp women exchanged uneasy nods.

Doc said, "Kate, you know the Earps."

Kate nodded.

They sat down as Fred White entered with Mayor John Clum and his wife. Fred White said, "Wyatt, this is Mayor Clum and his wife. Mayor, this is Wyatt Earp."

The mayor looked impressed. He said, shaking hands with Wyatt, "Mr. Earp, your reputation precedes you. I wonder . . ."

Wyatt smiled slightly. "Not a prayer. Nice meeting you."

While the orchestra was tuning up and the crowd's excitement was rising, Fred White sat next to Wyatt, pointing out the different cowboys and giving a thumbnail sketch of each. He said, "Well, just about everybody's here. We got the blades, the young blades. That would be Billy Claibourne, Wes Fuller, Tom and Frank McLaury, Ike and Billy Clanton. Billy is the youngest, the wild one.

"Then there is Frank Stillwell. There beside Curly Bill, that's Billy Breakenridge. Follows the cowboys around like a puppy. And then we've got the big boys. Curly Bill Brocius, he's the ramrod." He paused. "That's Johnny Ringo, best gun alive, they say." He stopped and smiled slightly at Wyatt Earp. "At least that's what they say. He's kinda different."

Wyatt said, "How different?"

Fred White shrugged. "Kinda hard to say. I reckon you've got to find out for yourself. Anyways, he's kinda the strange one. Curly Bill is the only one that he talks to. I mean they are all rough boys, but Ringo, I don't know. I really don't know."

The music suddenly came up and the houselights dimmed. The first act up on the bill was a juggler, dressed in parti-colored silks. As he came on stage and started his act, throwing Indian clubs into the air, one of the cowboys groaned. He said, "Oh hell, I seen him in Brisbee. All he does is catch stuff."

Another cowboy, Frank Stillwell, stood up and yelled, "Hey, Professor, catch this." With a swift motion, he drew his revolver and aimed at the whirling Indian clubs. He fired. One of the Indian clubs exploded before it was six inches out of the professor's hands. There were screams and scattered laughter in the audience. The professor was frozen in utter shock, he stared at the bullet in his hand.

He cried out, "They shot me. I don't believe it."

Without pause, he turned and bolted off the stage, passing Fabian, who was set to go on. The juggler said, "They are actually shooting at us. What will we do?"

Fabian said calmly, "Well, we won't have to wait for our notices."

They quickly announced Fabian's act, "Selections from the Bard by Mr. Romulus Fabian, Tragedian in Exclesis." The spotlight swung over as Fabian stepped out, a purple velvet cloak wrapped resplendently about him like a toga. He threw open his cloak and revealed his lithe form in doublet and tights.

The whores in the gallery began to hoot and cheer.

Curly Bill said, "Prettiest man I ever saw."

Another of the cowboys said, "How come he ain't wearin' no pants?"

Curly Bill laughed and pointed back to the whores and said, "That's how come."

As Fabian emoted, the crowd was restless at first and then quieted as his recitation began to take effect. He finished with:

"We few, we happy few, we band of brothers;
   For he today that sheds his blood with me
   Shall be my brother; be he ne'er so vile,
   This day shall gentle his condition;
   And gentlemen in England now abed
   Shall think themselves accurs'd they were not here,
   And hold their manhood cheap whiles and speaks
   That fought with us upon Saint Crispin's day!"

The cowboys were on their feet, cheering. They broke into wild applause. Fabian bowed elaborately.

Curly Bill said, "That's some feat. That's our kinda stuff."

The curtain fell. When it rose again, a backdrop had been put into place, revealing a wild painted scene of black and red, covered with weird designs and images of death and damnation.

An ancient white-bearded scholar sat alone with his books. Suddenly a hooded Satan danced across the stage, slender and lissome in paneled black doublet and breeches, tempting the old man with images of wealth and youth in the form of a shimmering ballerina who danced across the stage.

The audience watched in rapt attention.

Frank Stillwell said, "He's gonna come up short on that one."

Curly Bill said, "Know what I'd do? I'd take the deal, then crawfish and drill that ol' devil in the ass. How 'bout you, Johnny? What would you do?"

It was a moment before Johnny Ringo answered. Finally, he said, almost in a whisper, "I already did it."

Back on stage, Satan danced over the old man, exultant and triumphant, ready to collect the debt as the curtain fell with a final crashing chord from the orchestra. There was thunderous cheering and applause. The curtain rose again and the performers came out for bows, all except Satan.

In the box, Doc said dryly, "Very instructive."

Wyatt Earp, his eyes riveted on the stage, said, "But who was the devil?"

Suddenly Satan bounded out, removing the hood. The audience gave a gasp. It was Josephine Marcus.

With a start, Morgan Earp said, "Why, it's that woman from the coach."

Wyatt said, "Well, I'll be damned."

From the stage, Josephine spotted Wyatt's box and smiled. Her eyes locked in with his. Doc raised an eyebrow. He said, "You may indeed, if you get lucky."

The Earps, all six of them, strolled homeward. They gazed at the full moon and the beautiful night sky. Morgan said, "Boy, look at all those stars. Kinda makes you think, you know? God made all that, but He still remembered me. Wyatt, you believe in God?"

Wyatt said, "Yeah, maybe. Hell, I don't know."

"What do you think happens when you die?" said Morgan.

"Got me. Something. Nothin'. I don't know."

Morgan said, "I read this book on spiritualism—"

Virgil interrupted. "Oh God, here he goes. . . ."

"Said a lot of people, when they're dyin', they see this light. Say it's the light leadin' you to heaven."

Wyatt said, "Really? What about hell? They got a sign for that too?"

Morgan looked serious. "Hey, Wyatt, I am not kiddin'. You've got to take something like this serious."

Wyatt ignored him. He said, "Comin' to the Oriental, Virge?"

Allie answered for her husband. She said, "Not tonight. Tonight me and my old man're gonna have some fun. Get moving, old man."

She laughed, shoving Virgil down the street. He looked at Wyatt. "Her maiden name was Sullivan."

Wyatt and Mattie were alone now. The others had walked on ahead. Wyatt leaned down and kissed her on the cheek. He said, "Better go with them, honey. This is where I leave you."

Mattie grabbed his hand. She said, almost desperately, "No, please stay with me."

"Honey, I've gotta start makin' some money."

For a long moment Mattie just looked at him. Then, with a sigh of resignation, she said, "Oh, all right."

Wyatt hesitated. He said, "Well, I guess I don't have to go right now. I could stay awhile."

"No, no, I don't want to keep you."

"No, really, I can stay awhile."

"Just go. It's all right." Mattie bit her lip; her hands were shaking. "Wyatt, really, work well, make some money, don't worry about me."

Wyatt stared down at her for a long moment, but all he

could really see was the shining face of Josephine Marcus. He said slowly, "All right, well, good night."

He leaned down and gave her another kiss and headed down toward the Oriental. Behind him, Mattie's hand slowly stole into her purse, fishing for a bottle of laudanum.

Even at the late hour, the Oriental Saloon was packed, with the main draw being Wyatt Earp, dealing. At a break in the game, Wyatt relaxed in his chair. Doc Halliday was sitting across from him.

Doc said, "Well, tell me, Wyatt, do you actually consider yourself a married man. I mean, forsaking all others?"

"People change, Doc. I mean, sooner or later, people have to grow up."

Doc looked at his friend, trying to gauge the veracity of the statement and said, "I see. And now what would you do if she walked in here right now?"

Wyatt said, "Who's she?"

Doc laughed. "You know damned well who I mean. That dusky-hued lady Satan."

"I don't know, probably ignore her."

"Ignore her?"

"I'd ignore her. People can change, Doc."

"I'll remember that you said that."

He lifted his finger and pointed toward the door. Wyatt turned. Josephine had just walked in with the other actors.

Wyatt said, "Oh hell."

Josephine spotted Wyatt and started toward him, but he quickly looked away, as if ignoring her. She stopped. Sheriff Behan stepped up to her, tipping his hat gallantly. With another glance toward Wyatt, Josephine allowed herself to be led toward the bar.

Wyatt looked at Doc and said, "Satisfied?"

Doc said, "I stand corrected, Wyatt. You are an oak."

Just then, Mr. Fabian entered, dramatically gotten up like Lord Byron. There was a general commotion around him with Billy Breakenridge leading the way. But the actor turned from the throng and walked to a back table imperiously, his gaze sweeping around the room in noble triumph.

Doc said, "Reckon he don't ever take off his stage makeup?"

Wyatt laughed.

While Wyatt and Doc were talking, Curly Bill along with Ringo and the drunken Ike Clanton suddenly loomed over the empty faro table. Wyatt glanced up.

Curly Bill said, "Wyatt Earp, huh? I heard of you."

Ike Clanton, obviously drunk, said, "Listen, Mr. Kansas Law-dog. Law don't go around here."

Wyatt looked at the man. "I'm retired."

Curly Bill said, "That's good. That's real good."

"Yeah, that's good, Mr. Law-dog, 'cause law don't go around here."

Wyatt stared back at him. He said, "I heard you the first time, Ike."

Curly Bill said, "Shut up, Ike."

Ringo stepped up to the table. He had been hanging back. He said softly, "Then you must be Doc Holliday."

Doc smiled that mysterious smile of his and said, "That's the rumor."

"You retired too?"

Doc said, "Not me. I'm in my prime."

Ringo looked at him with his dead eyes. He said, "Yeah, you look it."

Kate made her way through the crowd and up to Doc's chair. She put her hand on his shoulder.

Doc said, "And you must be Ringo. Look, darling,

Johnny Ringo. The deadliest pistoleer since Wild Bill, they say. What do you think, darling? Should I hate him?"

Kate said, "You don't even know him."

He said, "Yes, but there's just something about him. Something about the eyes, I don't know, reminds me of . . . me. No, I'm sure of it, I hate him."

Wyatt spoke up to Ringo. "Don't mind what he said, he's drunk."

Doc looked into Ringo's eyes and said, *"In vino veritas."*

Ringo answered him back in Latin, *"Age quod agis."*

Doc said, *"Credat Judaeus Apella."*

With his dead eyes, Ringo patted his gun. He said, still speaking Latin, *"Eventus stultorum magister."*

The Cheshire-cat smile was back on Doc's face. He said meaningfully, *"In pace requiescat."*

Fred White had come up and said appeasingly, "Come on now, we don't want any trouble, not in any language."

Doc laughed. "Evidently, Mr. Ringo is an educated man. Now I really hate him."

For a long moment Ringo stared at Doc, holding his gaze while suddenly whipping out his revolver. Everyone but Doc flinched. Ringo did a dazzling series of twirls and tricks, his nickel-plated pistol flashing like a blaze of silver fire, finally slapping it back into his holster with a flourish.

There were cheers and hoots. Doc rolled his eyes, hooked his finger through the handle of his silver cup, then launched into an exact duplication of Ringo's routine, using his cup instead of his gun. The room burst into laughter. Ringo let a strange little hint of a smile cross his face, then he exited with the others.

When they were gone, White exhaled slowly. Then he turned to Wyatt. He said, "Wyatt, I'm gonna be old before my time, much more of this stuff happens."

Wyatt said, "Curly Bill, huh? Who was that other idiot?"

"Ike Clanton. Knows he ain't got the stuff, makes him miserable."

Wyatt said, looking at the departing party, "Yeah, and dangerous."

Across the room, Josephine sat at the bar watching the show. She turned to Behan and said, "The man dealing faro, what is his name?"

Behan said, "That's Wyatt Earp. Made quite a name for himself as a peace officer in Kansas."

Josephine let her eyes rest on the face of Wyatt Earp a long time. She said, "A peace officer . . . impressive man."

Ike and Curly Bill and Ringo were standing in the middle of the town. Even as late as it was, all the saloons were still going full blast. Ike shifted restlessly. He said, "I'm going to the Crystal Palace."

Curly Bill said, "You boys go ahead. Think I'll stick around awhile and howl at the moon."

Ike walked across the street. Ringo shrugged and walked off in a different direction.

Only Curly Bill remained, looking across the street. He was looking at a simple wooden building. Chinese laborers moved in and out; occasionally a white miner walked out, stoned on the opium they sold within. For a moment Curly Bill seemed to deliberate. Then he said, "Yeah, let's get woolly. I believe I'll have me some of what them Chinamen are using."

The Oriental Saloon was about to close. Only a few patrons remained. Doc was at the piano, drunk as a lord, but playing Chopin flawlessly. Kate poured him another drink.

She said, "That's my loving man, just can't get enough."

Doc smiled up at her and said, "Enough, never."

Now Billy Clanton came reeling in, loud and gratingly drunk. "Hey, is that 'Old Dog Tray'? Sounds like 'Old Dog Tray.'"

Doc said, "What?"

Billy Clanton staggered up to the piano. He said, "Do you know Stephen Foster. You know, 'O Susanna,' 'Camptown Races,' Stephen stinkin' Foster."

Doc said, "I see. Well, this happens to be a nocturne."

Billy Clanton stared at him. "A which?"

Doc said, "You know, Fréderic fucking Chopin."

Doc played on.

At the empty faro table, Morgan sat with Wyatt watching as the last few people left the saloon. Wyatt's eyes were on Josephine, where she sat with John Behan at a table near the door. As they watched, Josephine got up, Behan rising with her. They started for the door.

Morgan sighed. He said, "Why, that wounds me. Little tin swain walkin' off with that black beauty. I mean I'm a married man and all, but it still ain't right."

Wyatt looked away as Josephine and Behan left the saloon. He was obviously perturbed, trying not to show it. Just then, everyone jumped as gunshots echoed from outside. Fred White and Mayor Clum ran to the window.

Fred White said, peering through the pane of glass, "It's Curly Bill. He's across the street, shootin' out the lights."

The mayor swore for a moment. Then he said, "This is just great. This is just wonderful. Oh hell."

Just then Sheriff Behan walked in, white as a sheet. Josephine came in just behind him.

Behan said, "Have you been out in the streets: somebody's got to do something."

Mayor Clum said, "You're the sheriff."

Behan said insistently, "It's not county business. It's a town matter. It's out of my jurisdiction."

Out in the street, Curly Bill was floating. He had his head thrown back, luxuriating in the feel of the night air. His skin was alive. His brain was whirling. He felt the grit on the back of his eyelids. The opium smoke had done its job well.

Curly Bill yelled, "Boy, I feel great. I feel just . . . wonderful. Capital . . ."

Then, noticing the small audience gathering on the boardwalk, he began to take his potshots at their feet, causing them to scurry off dancing down the street.

He laughed loudly.

Inside the saloon, Fred White turned uneasily to Wyatt Earp and said, "Wyatt?"

Wyatt said, "Why don't you just leave it alone?"

Fred White gnawed at his lip. He said, "Naw. Gotta do something. I don't suppose you'd care. . . ."

Wyatt said, "None of my business, Fred."

He started to shuffle the cards in his hands. Doc kept on playing the piano. White started slowly toward the door.

Outside, Curly Bill reloaded his revolver and kept on shooting. There was a feeling of tension in the air, a feeling of terror. Fred White drew his gun with his trembling hand. He crossed the street and came up behind Curly Bill and said hesitantly, "Hey, Curly? Come on now, boy, we can't have this."

"Why don't you get out of bed?" Curly Bill spat out as he spun around. White's gun was staring him in the face.

He said, "Well, howdy, Fred."

Back inside the bar, Wyatt slowly put his cards down and looked over at Doc and said, "Maybe I ought to go out there."

Doc said, "Well, either you will or you won't. Don't look at me. I'm going to sleep."

Doc laid his head on the keys and passed out. Wyatt frowned for a moment. Finally, he stood up and turned to Morgan.

He said, "I guess you had better go wake up Virgil."

He turned to Joyce. He said, "Hey, Milt. Lend me a sidearm, will ya?"

From under the bar, the proprietor of the Oriental Saloon handed him a Colt .44.

Outside, White trembled visibly now. Perhaps because of his age, he looked almost frail, so vulnerable. Even his voice had a quavering edge to it. He said to Curly Bill, "Now hand that gun over."

Curly Bill said, "Well sure, Dad. I'm only having fun. Here she is."

With a reassuring smile, Curly Bill held his pistol out, butt first. White reached for it, visibly relieved. But quick as a snake's tongue, Curly Bill shifted it around and caught it by the butt and fired point-blank into Frank's chest, blowing him over backward, the blast so close that it set his clothes on fire.

Curly Bill turned just as Wyatt came out of the saloon and rushed over across the street. Before the cowboy could react, Wyatt slammed him across the head with his pistol barrel and laid him out in a groaning heap.

Wyatt glanced at White. He lay semiconscious in the street, chest heaving, eyelids fluttering, making weak little birdlike sounds, smoke rising from his smoldering shirt and vest. Clum came running up.

Wyatt said, "Put his clothes out."

Clumsily, Mayor Clum tried to put the embers out on White's clothes. But as Wyatt started to haul Curly Bill up, he suddenly found himself faced with an angry crowd of miners.

They yelled, "Get a rope. String him up."

Wyatt said, "No, you can't have him. I'm bringing him in."

Wyatt managed to drag the drunken Curly Bill to his feet and started to push him through the angry crowd on the street. Wyatt held up his hand. He suddenly found himself in front of Ike and six other cowboys as they surrounded him.

Ike said, "You turn loose of him."

Wyatt faced him calmly. He said. "He just killed a man."

Billy said, "Ike said to turn loose of him."

Wyatt glanced at him. "Well, I'm not letting you have him either."

The cowboys were still surrounding him, tensed up, ready for action. Ike said, "Swear to God, Law-dog, step aside or we'll tear you apart."

Ike stepped up almost in Wyatt's face. Suddenly, without warning, Wyatt jabbed the muzzle of his pistol into the cowboy's forehead, snapping his head back. Wyatt cocked the pistol. It made a deadly *clitch-clatch* sound as the hammer came back. The cowboys became quiet. Ike froze. Wyatt's eyes bored into him. Wyatt said, "You die first, you get it? The others might get me in a rush, but before that, I'm gonna make your head into a canoe. Understand?"

Across the street on the porch of the Grand Hotel, Josephine and Behan watched the standoff. Josephine's eyes were glued to Wyatt's.

Ike stood stock-still. A bead of sweat ran down his forehead. Billy suddenly ran forward and said, undaunted, "He's bluffin'. Let's rush him."

"No, he ain't," Ike said, trembles in his voice. "Don't make no sudden moves."

The other cowboys stopped and began to retreat. Then a voice from behind the crowd said in a slow manner, "Well, Billy boy, you music lover. Maybe you gonna be next. Maybe I'll make a canoe out of your head."

The crowd parted to admit Doc's thin frame. He stepped to Wyatt's side, his .38-caliber Lightning in his left hand. With his right hand he drew his big .45 Colt revolver.

Doc Holliday stood just behind Wyatt. Billy sneered. "Hell, he can't hit nothin'. He's so drunk, he probably can't hit nothin'. He's so drunk, he's probably seeing double."

Doc pulled out his .45, training it, too, on Billy. "Now I have two guns. If I am seeing double, then I have a gun for both of you," he said.

Billy paused. Suddenly there was another commotion as Virgil and Morgan bulled their way through the crowd. Both were carrying shotguns.

Virgil said, "All right, look out. Break it up. Go home, all of you, go home now. . . ."

This broke the group's will and they slowly began to disperse. Wyatt lowered his pistol and started forward with the still-groggy Curly Bill.

Wyatt said, "Come on, you. . . ."

Curly Bill said, "Crack me back of the head like some stinkin' bull. Hell, you ain't no fightin' man, you're just a cop."

They crossed the street. Curly Bill still stumbled as Wyatt steered him toward the jail.

Chapter Six

It was now morning at the Oriental Saloon. At the bar, Wyatt stood with Milt Joyce, counting money and making notations in the ledger book. As they worked he talked to his two brothers, who were playing pool at a table nearby.

He said, "But he says, 'Did I actually see it happen?' and I said, 'No, when I arrived, Fred had already been shot,' so the judge said, 'Can't have a murder without a witness. Case dismissed.' Can you believe that?"

Wyatt grimaced. "Oh hell, who cares, none of my business anyhow."

Virgil looked over at him, a certain coolness in his look. Then Morgan said as he lined up a billiard shot, "Boy, I love this game. When we finally get set, we gotta each have a billiards room in our houses."

Wyatt closed the bag of money and handed it to Milt Joyce, who took it and left the room. Wyatt took a few steps toward the pool table and leaned over toward Virgil.

Wyatt said, "Ya know, I was thinkin' that maybe we ought to open up our own place. That's the real money. Build it up, milk it for all it's worth, then sell it off for a bundle and breeze out of this burg with more money than Croesus and ready to live like kings."

Virgil just stood there. He did not respond.

Wyatt said, "Virge, let's you and me take a walk around town and see if we can scout us out a couple of nice lots."

"That what it's come down to for you, Wyatt? Making a lot of money? Is that what you've come to be?" Virgil asked.

"What's wrong with that, Virgil? What's wrong with that? Haven't we given enough?"

Virgil just shrugged and looked away. Morgan was still excited. He said, "I can't hardly believe it. It's working out just like you said, Wyatt. Were lootin' this burg six ways through Sunday."

Wyatt smiled. "Pretty good fun, too, ain't it?"

"Kinda, actually, yeah. I gotta admit it."

There was a loud noise as Virgil's cue landed on the floor. Whether he had dropped it or thrown it was not clear, but there was a set expression on his face. He turned away from Wyatt's glance, but it was apparent that he was not happy.

Just before words could be said, Mayor Clum entered, frowning and anxious. He said, coming up to the Earp brothers, "Excuse me, Wyatt, just a moment, please. I want to try and reason with you. We still haven't found a marshal to replace Fred and—"

Morgan cut him off. He said, "Come on, Mayor, he already told you no."

Wyatt said, "You tell him, Morgan."

But Clum didn't want to give up. He stared at Virgil. He said, "What about you, Virgil? You were a lawman. A federal lawman. A deputy United States marshal."

Virgil flicked his eyes away from the others. "I'm busy.

I'm busy, dammit, making money, dammit. Sorry, Mayor, but you're really barkin' up the wrong tree, dammit."

Wyatt smiled slightly. He gave Clum a look. He said, "Give you your answer?"

Clum started for the door and then he stopped and looked back. "You know, you men are making a lot of money in this town. Good for you, but a lot of decent people are suffering." He shrugged. "That's all I have to say."

When they were alone, Virgil looked at Wyatt. He said quietly, "Looks like you've strayed a long way off your range, Wyatt."

Wyatt bristled. "Now what the hell is that supposed to mean?"

"Just whatever you want it to mean."

All of a sudden a stable boy entered the saloon, looking around. He said to the men, "Mr. Earp? Mr. Wyatt Earp?"

Wyatt said, "Yeah, that's me."

"They told me to come tell you that Billy Clanton done stole your big stud horse and saddle last night."

Wyatt stiffened and said to Virgil, "Give me your gun belt, will ya?"

Virgil took off his gun belt and handed it to Wyatt. As Virgil was unbuckling it he said to Wyatt, "Now, don't go lookin' for trouble."

"I'm not looking for trouble, I'm just going to get my horse back."

He turned and started for the door.

Virgil called after him, "There was a day when you'd be just as interested, Wyatt, in getting the other man's horse back as you would have your own. That was when you were a lawman, remember?"

Wyatt gave him one long searching look, then turned and

went out the door, adjusting the gun belt as he did. The door slammed to behind him.

It was almost as if Billy Clanton was leaving a trail for him. Everyone that Wyatt asked on his way out of town had seen Billy Clanton with a big black horse.

The last man pointed him toward a small rise of hills and said that it was the direction that Billy Clanton had taken when he had ridden off into the desert.

It didn't much matter to Wyatt if Billy was leaving him a trail. If the young man wanted a showdown, then a showdown he would have.

Wyatt's heart was already troubled. True, the three brothers had agreed to give up the law to seek their fortunes, to give more of their lives to their wives, to make more money, to enjoy life. But it just didn't feel natural to Wyatt to stand by while others were getting hurt, and he could see the same thing in Virgil's eyes, even more than he was feeling it himself. He hadn't talked to Morgan, but he knew probably the same thoughts were running through Morgan's head.

He rode across the flat desert plain. The prints of a man riding a horse and leading a horse were clear to his eyes. There was no doubt that Billy Clanton was leading him straight toward the little row of purple-colored hills in the distance.

About a mile from the hills, he came to a small watering hole. A man was standing there on the ground while his horse watered.

Wyatt rode up to him and said, "Have you seen a man leading a black Morgan stallion?"

"I might've."

Wyatt said, "Well, either you did or you didn't. But the trail leads right here to your watering hole."

He waited for an answer, but none was forthcoming.

He said, "Oh, I see. So you must have been a cowboy, right? Really got you people treed, don't they?"

"Look, mister, it's fine for you boomers to court trouble, you're just passin' through. Us cattlemen gotta live here. Best I can do's point you up to the cut. That's their roost. But if I was you, ain't a horse alive would be worth me going up there after."

Wyatt said, "Reckon you ain't me."

As he got to the low line of hills, he could plainly see a cut going through their middle. A canyon with sheer walls was on both sides. It was the only entrance. With caution and determination, he advanced into it. He moved slowly, letting the rented stable horse just amble forward, watching for movement.

He was a couple hundred yards up the cut, the canyon climbing slowly, when a horseman suddenly seemed to materialize out of the sheer face of the cliffs. He came riding up to Wyatt.

"Run for your lives, boys, it's the bad lawman."

Wyatt looked at the man as he came riding up. He wasn't armed; at least he didn't have weapon in his hand.

Wyatt said, "McMasters, ain't it? Listen, you seen a black stallion with—"

McMasters said, "Listen, I got a rule. I don't talk to lawmen. Dogcatchers neither."

"I'm not a lawman, just a private citizen trying to get my property back."

McMasters laughed. "Well, in that case, I saw your horse. Billy Clanton was taking him to the cut to show him off. The boys are all up there now branding, and boy, are they ever in a mood. Are you sure you still want your property back, Mr. Private Citizen?"

Wyatt just glanced at him and urged his horse forward. McMasters fell in alongside of him. As they rode up to the crown of the hill, Wyatt said, "So what about you cowboys anyway?"

McMasters said, "If I had to explain it, you wouldn't understand. Just say we're brothers. To the bone."

"Yeah, but some of the things that they say your brothers have done . . ."

"There's all kinds of horses, ain't there? And all kinds of dogs, ain't there? Same with cowboys. What they do's their affair. I don't preach and I don't judge. I ain't no dogcatcher either, like some I could name."

They suddenly topped a rise at the height of the little hills and a wide plateau opened before them, dyed with tents, water and feed troughs, small shacks, and campfires scattered here and there. There were cattle there along with some horses.

Some of the cowboys were busy with the business of rebranding steers while others sat around cooking, drinking, or just talking. They looked up with naked hostility as Wyatt rode up. McMasters pointed toward the edge of camp where Billy was standing with Wyatt's stallion.

McMasters said, "There he is, if you want 'em bad enough."

Wyatt saw his stud. Billy stood next to it.

McMasters said, "You seem like a nice enough fella. Like to've known you better, had you lived."

Wyatt started riding straight for Billy. From behind the black horse, Ike Clanton and an Indian named Hawk Swilling suddenly stepped forward. All three of them were facing Wyatt.

Ike said, "Hey, Law-dog. What the hell you doin' here?"

Swilling said, "How about I just drag you off that horse and eat you blood raw?"

Wyatt ignored them. Coming to a stop ten feet from Billy, he sat there looking at Billy and then quickly dismounted.

Billy stood there supremely confident and unconcerned.

Wyatt stepped forward and said, "Where'd you get that horse?"

Billy said, "Beauty, ain't he?"

Almost casually, Wyatt brushed back the skirt of his coat so that it freed his gun butt. He said, "I asked where you got him?"

"Where do you think? I stole him."

The other cowboys had come around. Wyatt took several more steps toward Billy. Now they all laughed. He said, "I want my horse back."

With a sudden move, Billy pulled an enormous bowie knife from behind his back. He said, "Well then, come and get him."

Wyatt stopped and took a long, slow look around at all the men. They all stared back. Wyatt ignored the knife in Billy's hand and sighed. He said, "Okay. Let's go, boy."

Wyatt and Clanton began to move toward each other as the cowboys looked on excitedly, placing their bets on who would win. Just as Wyatt and Billy were about to clash, Curly Bill suddenly streaked through the crowd on his buckskin mare, majestic and as if ten times life-size. As he skidded to a stop in front of Wyatt, he raised a giant rooster tail of dust, making everyone but Wyatt recoil.

Curly Bill said in a hard voice, "Give him his horse, Billy."

Ike stepped forward. He said, "Now you stay outta this, Curly—"

"Shut up, Ike," said Curly Bill.

"You don't talk to me like that. My old man started this gang. I should be runnin' the show."

Curly Bill looked at him and said, "You ain't got enough in your britches. You think you can prove otherwise, go ahead."

There was long silence as Ike stared at Curly. Finally, he began to wilt. He said, "I don't have to take this."

But then he suddenly walked back to his horse and rode off.

Now at the center of the cowboys' circle, there was just Curly Bill, Billy, and Wyatt Earp.

Curly Bill said, "Give him the horse, Billy."

Another long second passed and then Billy slowly handed the bridle over to Wyatt.

Curly Bill said, "Frank, Tom, go after Ike and cool him off. The rest a' you get back to work."

Finally, there was no one standing there except Curly Bill and Wyatt. Curly Bill said, as if in explanation of his actions, "I feel bad about ol' Fred. I just can't hold back when I'm feelin' kinda woolly. I know I ought to leave that silly smoke alone that you get in that Chinese joint, but sometimes I just get it comin' on me. Still, I feel kinda bad. But now we're square. Anyway, no use for holdin' a grudge. I deserved that rap in the head you gave me."

Wyatt said, "I'll make you a deal. Me and my brothers want to settle down in Tombstone. You and your boys stay out of our way, and I'll make sure we stay out of yours."

Curly Bill answered, "Fair enough."

Wyatt said, "Tell me one thing."

"What?"

Wyatt said, "They were all going to jump me back there. Whatever happened to one-on-one?"

Curly Bill smiled and said, "Ain't our way, we go all on

one, and one on all. You fight one of us, you fight all of us. That's the cowboy way."

"Then how come you call yourselves cowboys? Cowhands ride for a brand."

"Oh, we ride for a brand all right."

He gave Wyatt the finger.

"This brand. How about you?" Curly Bill asked.

Wyatt said, pointing his finger to his chest, "I ride for this brand."

Curly Bill nodded. He said, "Well, sir, we're gonna get along just fine, then."

Josephine Marcus had chosen to take a ride in the desert in the cool of the midmorning. She was gorgeously dressed in an impressive black velvet riding habit and rode sidesaddle through the plains on a pretty little mare.

Suddenly she saw movement just ahead in a small grove of trees. Apprehensively, she halted her horse as she watched a horseman emerge from the trees heading straight toward her. For an instant she was about to start her horse and ride back to town some two miles away.

But just then she recognized the set of the shoulders and the way he carried his head and knew it was Wyatt Earp.

Her heart, in spite of her, gave a quick little bound. She sat watching him as he came toward her.

Wyatt had recognized Josephine before she recognized him, and his heart, too, gave a slight little bound. He had tried to make himself think of Mattie, the Mattie who had stuck by him, the Mattie whom he knew he had driven to the laudanum. Yet even as he neared Josephine Marcus he could feel the tearing inside him, he could hear the beating of his heart. He did not want to be unfaithful. He did not want to turn his back on Mattie.

As he approached Josephine with no idea of what might happen, he was already feeling tormented, guilty. But at the same time, he could no more turn away from her than a man dying of thirst could have turned away from the salvation of a water well.

As he rode up to her he took his hat off with a sweeping gesture. He said, "How do you do, madam? Didn't expect to find a lady like you out here in the great nowhere. You be the lady from the actors' troupe?"

She smiled, almost breaking his heart, and said, "And you would be Wyatt Earp, the famous lawman."

"No, ma'am. I'd be Wyatt Earp, the faro dealer."

He smiled and continued, "How is it, ma'am, that you would know the name of such a poor one as me?"

"It isn't by chance that I should know your name," she replied boldly, "because I asked, Mr. Earp. I was beginning to think we would never meet in person. This is fortuitous. That means lucky."

"I know what it means. I just ain't so sure how lucky it is."

Before she could answer, Wyatt's stallion groaned nervously and threw his head back, aroused by the presence of the mare.

"Easy now. Your mare is in season," he said.

She said, "Oh."

Wyatt patted his horse, trying to calm him. He said, "Your mare has just started. It would be worse if it was just a little farther along."

Josephine said, "But how do they know?"

"They know. It's the scent." He smiled slightly. She, too, had a scent.

"We'd better split them up."

Josephine said, "I've got a better idea. Let's run it out of them."

Before Wyatt could stop her, she was off at a full gallop. Wyatt paused for a moment, debating with himself. Finally, he said, "Yeah, I'm an oak, all right."

He laid spurs to his horse and took off at a dead run. In a hundred yards, he had caught Josephine on her mare. He rode up alongside of her, his stallion setting his rhythm to that of the smaller mare.

Coming off a rise, the desert floor sheared off into a wide crevice. Josephine was heading right at it.

Wyatt yelled over the wind, "You're not that crazy, are you?"

Josephine was leaning forward in the saddle, getting ready. "Oh, yes I am."

She cracked her horse with her crop and streaked toward the crevice. Wyatt gritted his teeth and followed suit. The sound of their hoofbeats stopped for a long instant as they took the jump together, sailing through the air side by side. Then they lit on the far side and galloped on, Josephine giggling like a little girl.

They finally pulled up at a beautiful grove of oaks, carpeted with wildflowers. Wyatt dismounted, helping Josephine down. He took his long duster from his saddle and laid it on the ground for them to sit on.

Josephine said, throwing back her beautiful head of hair, "Oh, that was lovely."

"You know that you almost got us both killed back there, don't you?"

"Fun, though, wasn't it?"

"You'd die for fun?"

"Wouldn't you? You're laughing. I was sure that you never laughed."

Wyatt tossed his head in annoyance. He had heard that all too often. He said, "I laugh sometimes."

"Yes, but how often?"

She looked into his eyes. "Tell me, are you happy?"

He thought for a moment. "Am I happy? I don't know. Happy as the next man, I guess. I don't laugh all day long like an idiot, if that's what you mean."

"You're a little touchy about it, aren't you?"

"I'm not touchy. It's just a silly question, that's all. Am I happy? Are you happy?"

Josephine reached out her slender finger and touched his cheek. She said, "Of course, I'm always happy, unless I'm bored. That blond woman, that your wife?"

Wyatt was suddenly defensive. He said, "What about her?"

"Nothing. Tell me, what do you want out of life?"

Wyatt laughed sharply. "Where do you get all these questions?"

Josephine said, stroking his cheek with just that one finger, "Just answer."

Wyatt said tiredly, "I don't know. Make some money, have some kids. You know."

Josephine shook her head. "That doesn't suit you."

Wyatt looked her in the face. "How would you know?"

"It just doesn't, that's all."

Wyatt said with a trace of irritation in his voice, "Well, I ought to know my own mind, and I'm tellin' you what suits me is a family and kids. That suits me right down to the ground. In fact, that's my idea of heaven."

Wyatt paused, his face working. He looked off in the distance. He said, "All right, what's your idea of heaven?"

Josephine laughed. She said, "Room service."

Wyatt laughed in spite of himself, shaking his head and looking rueful. He said, "You are some lady."

Josephine said, "See, you're laughing again. But that's what I want. To go places and move and never look back and just have fun. Forever. That's my idea of heaven. I need someone to share it with, though."

Wyatt frowned. He said, "You mean somebody like John Behan?"

She shrugged.

He said, "That why you are with him?"

"Well, he's handsome and he's charming. He's all right. For now. Don't say it, I know, I'm rotten. I can't help it, I've tried to be good, but it's too boring."

Wyatt shook his head and said, "The way you talk." He frowned. "Never heard a woman talk like that before."

Josephine said, tossing her hair, "Oh look, I haven't got time to be proper. I want to live. I'm a woman, I like men. If that's unladylike, well, I guess I'm not a lady. At least I'm honest."

Wyatt said slowly, "Well, you are different, there's no arguing that. But you're a lady all right. I'll take my oath on that."

He looked at her, enchanted, his heart bounding again, but then his face clouded.

Josephine instantly sensed the change in his mood. She said, "What's wrong?"

"I don't know. Doesn't make any sense. I almost can't look at you. Like it hurts."

Now her mood matched his. She said sadly, "I know, me too. What should we do about it?"

For a full moment they stared at each other. Then, almost as if against their will, they fell into each other's arms and then he kissed her.

77

She sank deeper into his embrace. He kissed her again, then fell to his knees, threw his arms around her legs, and pressed his face into the folds of her skirt.

Wyatt said, "God."

She ran her fingers through his hair. He suddenly stood up, lifted her with him until they were face-to-face. She could feel him pressing into her.

Josephine said, "You know this is adultery. You burn in hell for that."

Wyatt said through gritted teeth, "Then let's make sure we get our money's worth, dammit."

Chapter Seven

As Wyatt rode into Tombstone that night his mind and his heart were so full of Josephine Marcus that he didn't notice the commotion and tumult that was going on in town until he was almost in the middle of it.

There was a large group of men gathering around the jail. Some of them were holding torches like an old-fashioned political parade. Others were hammering notices to posts in front of buildings.

As he drew nearer he could hear a man's voice coming from the front of the crowd at the jail. It was a moment before he recognized it as Virgil's.

"Now, wait, nobody is saying that you can't own a gun, nobody's saying that you can't carry a gun. All we're saying is that you can't carry one in town. Now, that's not too much to ask, is it?"

There was a smattering of applause, a few catcalls from the crowd. Wyatt's eyes opened wide at the sight before him. Virgil was standing on the porch in front of the jail. He had just finished nailing up a proclamation, and as he turned he revealed a gleaming silver shield on his breast. He stood on a platform, Morgan at his side, holding a proclamation up to a crowd of townspeople in front of the jail.

Wyatt spurred his mount forward, forcing his way through the crowd. "What the hell are you doing?"

He dismounted and stepped up on the platform. He said, "I told you that we weren't gonna get involved."

Virgil stared back at him. He said, "But you got us involved. When you brought us here, you got us involved because you were Wyatt Earp."

Wyatt pointed a finger at Virgil. He said, "Now, you hold on here, Virge."

"Hold on nothin'. I looked around this town today and it was like someone slapping me in the face. These people're afraid to even walk down the street. Hell, they can't walk down the street. And I'm trying to make money off it like some kind of goddamn vulture. That's not me, that's somebody I don't even know."

Wyatt said, "We don't owe this town a thing."

Virgil said, "If we're gonna have a future here, this town has gotta be safe."

"Virgil, please don't do this to me."

"It's got nothing to do with you, Wyatt. It's got to do with—"

Wyatt cut him off. "Nothing to do with me? I'm your brother."

He turned to Morgan. He said, "Talk to him."

Morgan looked down in sheepish silence. Wyatt stared at him for a moment before he said, "Oh God, don't tell me. . . ." He let the thought trail off. Morgan pulled back his coat, revealing the deputy's badge on his vest. Wyatt cursed softly.

Morgan said, "Like you said, Wyatt. We're brothers. Gotta back your brother's play. Just like I figured you would."

Wyatt said, "Listen to me, both of you."

He reached out, took each of them by the vest, and pulled them toward him. He said, "You can't do this. We came here to make money. We got the best table in town."

Virgil said, "Yeah, that's because people want to say that they played faro against the famous Wyatt Earp."

Wyatt shook his head hard. He said, "No, no, no. They come to my game because they know it's a fair game."

Virgil just looked at him and said, "Wyatt, it's done. Make up your mind to it. Morgan and I are in."

Wyatt said anxiously, "Walk away from here, please. Just walk away from the crowd so I can talk to you."

Reluctantly, the two brothers followed him to the head of an alley. The lights from the torches flickered on all three of their faces. Wyatt said, "This is trouble that we don't need. For the first time in our lives, we got a chance to stop wandering and finally be a family. You saw what happened to Fred White."

Morgan said, "Come on, we're not about pickin' fights. Like Virgil said, you just gotta know how to handle 'em. Old Fred just wasn't up to it. We know what they're doing, Wyatt."

"All right, say you're right, say you don't get yourself killed. There's something else." Wyatt paused. "It's not too late for you, Morgan."

Morgan looked at him wearily. He said, "What are you talking about?"

Wyatt exhaled and then crouched down in front of his younger brother, looking deep into his eyes, his voice soft and plaintive. He said, "All the years I worked in the cowtowns, I was only ever mixed up in one shooting. A man lost his life and I took it. You don't know how that feels, Morgan. Believe me, boy, you don't ever want to feel that way. Not ever."

He paused, looking at his brother. "Didn't even make a dent, did I? You're both makin' a big mistake."

In the cottage they had rented, Mattie lay on the bed, half dozing, lost in an opium dream. In the dream, she was trying to chase Wyatt across the desert. He was riding slowly on a pale horse. Occasionally he would look back at her, struggling in the sand. Sometimes he would stop and she would almost reach him, her arms outstretched toward him. But then he would ride slowly on, leaving her behind.

She awoke out of the dream to the sound of the front door opening and closing. Then she heard Wyatt's unmistakable step as he walked into the bedroom. She watched him as he walked over and gave her a light kiss. He glanced at the almost empty laudanum bottle on the nightstand.

He said, "That the bottle Louisa gave ya?"

Mattie said almost defiantly, desperately, "I know what I am doing. Where have you been?"

He said evasively, "Oh, just out riding. Just looking the desert over. How are you doing?"

"I don't know. No, no, I'm all right. Really I am. You shouldn't worry about me. You've got enough on your mind."

Wyatt sat down on the edge of the bed, took her hand in his, and said, "Really, are you sure, Mattie, that you are all right?"

"Sure I'm sure. Say, what is this?"

Wyatt sat for a moment, thinking. Suddenly his face came alive.

"You know, we've already made a pile of money. I was just thinking that maybe we should pull up stakes and move on. We could stay on the move, you know. Just keep going, see the world and live on room service the rest of our lives. How'd that be?"

Mattie stared at him. She said, "Room service? Wyatt,

what are you talking about? When did we ever have room service?"

Wyatt shook his head. He said, "Oh, just forget it. Just thinking out loud. Forget it. Just got a little too much night air."

He thought a minute more and then got up. As he neared the door and turned to Mattie, he said, "Well, you'll hear about it soon enough, but Virgil and Morgan done got themselves up into trouble."

Mattie looked alarmed. "What do you mean?"

Wyatt just shook his head. "You'll find out soon enough."

At the door, he turned back and looked at her and said, "I'm gonna go on back out for a little bit. I shouldn't be too late."

She said, "Don't worry about me, Wyatt, I will be all right, honest. Have a good time. I mean it. You deserve a good time."

The Oriental Saloon was almost empty except for a poker game at a table in the back corner. There were six players, including Virgil, Morgan, Ike Clanton, the McLaurys, and Doc Holliday.

It was an odd group to be playing together. There was tension that hung over the table that was not caused by the large pots of money that were being bet.

Across the room, Josephine lounged against the piano, luscious in a white gown that showed off her figure at its best.

In a low sultry voice, she was singing "Frankie and Johnny." She glanced to her left as Wyatt entered. He stopped, startled at the sight of her. John Behan suddenly appeared at Wyatt's elbow.

Behan said, "Well, what do you think of the singer?"

Wyatt, with his eyes still focused on Josephine, said, "Nice voice."

He nodded weakly at her. She gave him a half smile in return. Wyatt blushed slightly.

He walked toward the game in the back, looking carefully over the players. As he approached, Morgan got up from the table and came toward him.

Morgan said, "Doc won't quit. He's been up for thirty-six hours, and Clanton came in an hour ago. They switched to poker. Tried to get him to bed, but he just won't let go."

Wyatt said, "What about Katie? Won't he listen to her?"

"Nope."

Wyatt shook his head. "I know. Nobody can make him do anything."

Wyatt walked slowly over to the table. Doc was sitting across the table from Ike Clanton. As he approached, Doc looked up and smiled that smile of his.

"Wyatt, just in time. Pull up a chair. Join us."

Wyatt said, "No thanks, Doc. A little late for me. I'm just not in the poker mood right now."

He glanced at Kate, who was standing behind Doc as she always did, the whiskey bottle in her hands, ready to refill the little silver cup, the only one that Doc would ever drink from. She shook her head slightly as Wyatt gave her a questioning look.

Wyatt watched as the cards were being dealt around the table. Over Doc's shoulder he could see that Doc had been dealt two pair, sixes and nines. The bets went around.

Virgil dropped out. The last raise was for one hundred dollars by Ike Clanton. Everybody dropped out except Doc and Frank McLaury. Doc raised the pot two hundred and McLaury dropped out.

Now there was only Ike Clanton and Doc Holliday playing. Virgil was dealing. He said to Ike Clanton, "How many cards?" Ike put two cards into the discard pile.

"Two. Two cards."

Virgil looked over at Doc. Doc made a show over whether to take one card or two. Obviously, he was going to try to draw to the two pair and try to make a full house.

Finally he discarded the fifth card, which was a queen. He held up one finger and in his best imitation of an imperial lord said, "Just the one lone soldier, if you will, my lord."

Silently, Virgil slid the card across the table to Doc. Wyatt watched as Doc picked the card up without looking at it, put it with the other four, and shuffled the cards together.

As he spread his hand Wyatt could see that Doc had drawn the other six, filling the full house.

Doc looked across at Ike Clanton, the dislike apparent in his eyes and his voice when he said, "I believe it's your bet, my fine fellow. My fine musical brother. No, excuse me. That's your brother, the young Billy."

Ike bristled. He said to Doc Holliday, "One of these days, mister, just one of these days."

Doc raised his eyebrows. "Yeah, one of these days, what? Mr. Ike Clanton. But meanwhile, this is not one of these days, this is this day, this hour, this minute, right now. It is your bet. Since you proposed the last bet, and I raised it, it is your bet. Or do you know the rules of poker, sir?"

Wyatt smiled at himself. He knew Doc's tricks. Doc was intentionally trying to infuriate the other man so that he would bet over his head, lose his head and his money. It seemed to be working.

Clanton said, "Damn you, you dried-up old lunger. I know the rules of poker better than any man alive. You wanna bet? Fine, I'll bet. Two hundred dollars. Now."

With his left hand, he counted out two hundred dollars in bills and shoved them into the pot. He said, "Now, how do you like those apples, old man?"

Doc smiled. He said, "Old man, is it? Dried-up lunger, is it?" He turned his head back toward Kate and said, "My love, a small libation is in order. I have just been called an old man and a dried-up old lunger. Perhaps whiskey will make it go down easier."

While Kate poured Ike Clanton raved. "Dammit, you calling or not? Are we here to play poker or drink whiskey, or can't you do both?"

To further infuriate him, Doc saluted him with the silver drinking cup. He said, "To your health. Not your luck, just your health." He drank off the whiskey and set the cup down.

He carefully counted out two hundred dollars and threw them into the pile.

He said, "How is that for a dried-up old lunger and an old man? Can a stalwart young buck like yourself match it?"

The fury was almost erupting out of Ike Clanton. He had completely lost his head. Without so much as a pause, he snatched his money up and threw it all in. "And that is ten dollars better. There is three hundred and ten dollars there."

Doc said, "Only too happy to oblige." With a delicate thumb and forefinger, he selected a ten-dollar bill from the pile and threw it in. "There you have it, sir."

Ike Clanton almost rolled out of his chair as he slammed his fist upon the table.

He said, "There, by God, beat them three aces, you old four-flusher."

Doc smiled cynically. Then, in an eloquent effeminate gesture, he slowly fanned his hand, one card at a time, until the full house was showing.

He said, "I believe I have."

Ike Clanton was almost out of his head with fury. He slammed both fists down on the table.

He said, "Son of a bitch, that's twelve straight hands. Nobody's that lucky."

Around the table, the Earps stiffened as the small catlike smile formed around Doc's face.

Doc said delicately, "Now, Ike, whatever do you mean?"

Virgil stood up. He said, "Come on, boys, take it easy. Let's don't have no trouble here."

But Doc was looking at Ike Clanton with his dead eyes, his words purposely provoking him. He said, "Maybe poker is not your game. Maybe we could have a spelling bee."

Ike Clanton was almost beside himself with rage. His friends were trying to restrain him. They were aware of Doc Holliday's reputation, but Ike Clanton was beyond remembering it.

He said, the words almost strangling him, "I'll wring your scrawny neck for you, you old bastard."

The McLaurys were trying to pull him away.

Virgil stepped in, pushing Clanton farther away from the table. "Now that's enough Clanton. That's enough. The hand's over."

Ike Clanton said, "You takin' his part? I'm the one was cheated. Goddamned pimps, you're all in it together."

He continued saying, "The son of a bitch cheated me. You know he cheated me."

Virgil had now had enough. He had hold of Clanton by both shoulders and said, "Nobody's in anything, Clanton. You're drunk. Go home and try to sleep it off." Virgil tried to push him farther back from the table.

Ike began trying to shove Virgil away. He said, "Get your goddamn hands off me. Don't you ever put your hands on one of us. Don't you ever try to manhandle a cowboy. We'll cut your goddamned pimp's heart out. Understand, pimp?"

Virgil said, "Don't you threaten me, you little . . ."

Violence hung in the air like a cloud. Wyatt hurried out from behind the table, jumping in between the McLaurys and Ike Clanton, separating all of them.

From across the room, Behan noticed Josephine gasp, a look of alarm crossing her face.

Wyatt said, "Whoa, whoa. Take it easy, boys. Ike, just go home and forget it, will you?"

Ike said, staring at Wyatt Earp, "I ain't forgetting nothing, I ain't forgetting a damned thing. I seen how you sided with that drunk, that lunger, that damned card cheat. Don't reckon this is gonna be forgotten. You may be Wyatt Earp in Dodge City, but you ain't shit here. You got that straight?"

A quiet settled over the barroom. All eyes turned toward Wyatt to see what his next move would be. He stood there, staring at Ike Clanton.

For a long second he gazed into Clanton's eyes. Gradually, little by little, Clanton wilted. One of the McLaurys said, "Oh, the hell with it, Clanton, let's get out of here. Let's go someplace else. This place gives me the willies."

The three of them turned and uncertainly made their way down the long room to the bar. There was a quiet for a few seconds then Doc said, "Well, that certainly was a bust. I want my money back." He turned to Kate and continued, "Come, darling. Let's seek out entertainment elsewhere."

Doc stood up, taking Kate's arm to leave. He took one step and fell back dizzily, suddenly breaking out in a sweat and coughing.

Kate said, "What's wrong, Doc? Doc, Doc, what's wrong?"

Doc righted himself. "Nothing, not a thing. I am as right as the mail."

Again, he tried to stand up. This time he keeled over onto the floor and started coughing up blood. Wyatt rushed to his side.

Kneeling by his friend's prone form, Wyatt said, "Get a doctor. Morgan, give me a hand."

Together, they lifted the unconscious Doc Holliday off the floor and laid him over the poker table.

At the bar at the very end of the saloon, Ike Clanton and his friends were having one last drink before going home. Ike asked Milt Joyce, "What's wrong with him?"

Milt Joyce said, "He's got consumption."

They watched as Virgil helped Morgan and Wyatt try to get Doc on his feet. Ike said, "I hope he dies. Bastard thinks he can cheat me."

Joyce said, "Nobody cheated you, Ike. Just go home."

Ike suddenly leaned over the bar and slapped Joyce in the face. Joyce scowled, more irritated than hurt. Ike said, "Give me my rifle." Without saying a word, Joyce reached under the bar and handed him his lever-action carbine.

To the McLaurys, Ike said, "See, give somebody a rap on the breezer and get some respect around here."

Ike was standing at the bar as Virgil, Morgan, and Wyatt helped Doc Holliday out into the night, headed for a doctor's office. They had already passed through the doors when Virgil suddenly reentered. Seeing the lawman, Ike drunkenly tried to put a round into the chamber of his rifle.

Without even a pause, Virgil slammed his heavy fist into Clanton's face, the rifle clattering to the floor. Virgil then grabbed him by the front of his shirt and started towing him toward the door.

He said, "Come on, you idiot."

The Earps had helped Doc to his room in the boardinghouse, where he lay on the bed, looking even smaller than he did when he was up and around. Kate leaned against the wall, watching him anxiously. They waited with him until the doctor came, and then Wyatt left.

The doctor leaned over Doc Holliday and examined him. He seemed to have revived, but he still looked very bad. The front of his shirt was stained with small patches of dried blood that he had coughed up. His mouth was gaping open, his eyes swimming with every breath.

The doctor finished his examination and straightened up, putting his jacket on while Kate watched apprehensively.

"Your condition is quite advanced. I'd say you've lost sixty percent of your lung tissue, maybe even more," the doctor said.

Doc said, "So what does that mean?"

The doctor shrugged and pulled a face. He said, "Two years, two days. If you stop now—I mean the drinking, gambling, nightlife. What I mean is you must attempt to deny your marital impulse."

Doc Holliday laughed. He said, "Well, that sounds inviting." He glanced at Kate. "Did you follow that?"

"No, I reckon not. What did the doctor say?"

As the doctor began gathering up his equipment Kate began rolling Doc a cigarette. She said, "How are you feelin'?"

He smiled at her and said, "Better. Of course, it is difficult to say. Better than what?"

"That's good. I knew it wasn't nothing, Doc. I've always known that."

For a moment Doc Holliday looked sad. He said, "We must talk, darling. It appears that we have to redefine the definition of our relationship."

Kate looked bewildered. She said, "What's that mean, Doc? You know I don't understand when you talk up high like that. You mean, you don't want to be my lovin' man no more?"

Doc said, "Well, not exactly. You don't understand what the good doctor said when he said among other things, I would have to control my marital impulse?"

Kate shook her head. "No, Doc, you know I don't understand any of that kind of stuff."

Doc smiled slightly. He said, "Well, someday, I will explain it to you better. You know what we do in bed?"

Kate said, "Well, we sleep and then we, well, you know."

Doc said, "It's that 'you know' that I'm talking about."

Kate's lower lip came out. She said, "But Doc, I'm a good woman to you. Don't I always take care of you? Nobody cares for you like me. I'm a good woman."

Doc said, "Yes, I know you are, Kate. You are a good woman."

Kate smiled, licking the cigarette that she had been rolling. She put it in Doc's mouth and leaned over to light it, making it so her ample bosom bulged over her body. Doc stared at her chest, something behind his eyes seeming to shut down.

Doc said, "Then again, you may be just one of my bad habits."

It was good morning in front of the Allen Street jail. The McLaurys were helping Ike through the jail door when Virgil and Morgan looked on.

Frank said, "Come on, Ike."

Tom said, "Ya gonna give Ike back his guns?"

"Not until he sobers up."

While Frank took Ike down the street Tom suddenly twirled to face the Earps and said, "Just who the hell do you think you are?"

Virgil said, "Right now, we are the law. And right now, you are getting dangerously close to breaking it."

Tom said, "Son of a bitch." He turned and started down the sidewalk, and almost bumped into Wyatt.

Tom said, "You stupid bastard, watch how you walk."

"Easy, son, I'm sorry."

Tom said, "I ain't easy and I ain't your kid and you can shove sorry up your ass, you pimp."

Tom stepped back, pulling open his coat, showing his pistol. Before he could reach for it, Wyatt snatched it and rapped him over the head with it. Tom fell to his hands and knees. Wyatt hit him again on the back of the neck and Tom fell flat. Then Wyatt dropped the gun on him as Ike and Frank ran up to them. Tom lay there. They tried to help him up, but he was too groggy to stand.

Ike turned to Wyatt, his eyes full of rage. He said, "Damn you, you're gonna bleed for that. You got a fight comin' and it's comin fast."

Wyatt stared at him for a moment. He said, "I thought I made it clear when I come here that I've quit fighting. But you boys keep pushing me and I might not be able to keep from fighting and you're liable to get your wish—only you might not want that wish once you get it."

Ike said, "All right, maybe today is not going to be the day. But the day is coming. You three Earps won't always be together, you can count on that. And you can count on your day coming."

With Ike's help, Frank McLaury helped Tom up and they staggered off down the sidewalk as Virgil and Morgan stepped out into the street.

Virgil turned and said in disbelief, "What the hell is going on here?"

Tom had recovered from the pistol whipping Wyatt had given him, but was still rubbing the back of his neck when he and Ike and Frank McLaury met up with Billy Clanton, Billy Claibourne, and Wes Fuller down near the Crystal Palace Saloon. They stood in a line in front of the jail.

Virgil looked down the street and said, "Now there's six

of 'em. This is like a bad dream. I don't know how things keep happening."

Wyatt said, "Just keep your head, it'll be all right. Just the same, though . . ." He paused and sighed and looked away. "Virgil, I thought I would never see the day that I would say this again. You're the deputy marshal here. You've sworn Morgan in. I guess it's finally come to it, I guess you had better swear me in."

Virgil and Morgan exchanged glances. Virgil said, "It's the only way, Wyatt. I know you feel bad about it, and you didn't ask for this trouble. But trouble's come and we're gonna have to deal with it. The Earps have never run from trouble, and I'm not gonna see this bunch of bullies running this town any longer. Having you with us will make all the difference."

Wyatt walked slowly into his cottage and into the parlor, where Mattie sat. On the side table was a brass-mounted wooden case. For a long moment he stared down at it.

Finally, he lifted the lid. It opened to reveal a gleaming Colt .45 with an extra-long barrel. A gold shield was inlaid on the burled walnut grips and engraved with the words, *To Wyatt Earp, Peacemaker*.

It was a gift from Ned Buntline, the famous western writer who had chronicled many of the adventures of the lawmen of the West. It was called the Buntline Special. It was Wyatt Earp's legendary sidearm.

Wyatt took it from the case and put it in his coat pocket as Mattie looked on. She said, "I thought you swore that you would never carry that thing again."

Wyatt looked at her and said, "Yeah, well, I swore a lot of things, Mattie. Things it looks like I can't keep."

He turned toward her said, "I can't run from their trouble. Would you have me do it?"

She knotted her hands in her lap and said, "Oh, Wyatt, who am I to tell anyone? Wyatt, I am so sorry that I have failed you. I am so sorry. I wanted to be a good wife to you. I wanted desperately to be a good wife to you. I am so sorry."

Wyatt crossed over to her and said, "Mattie, Mattie. Please don't think that. You are a good wife. I know that you have a little problem now, but you'll solve it. I know you will."

He gazed at her. He said, "Please don't make this any harder than it already is."

She put her hand up to his chest and smiled. She said, "Oh, I love you. Oh, how I love you. Please be careful. I don't want to lose you."

As he stood up he thought of Josephine, and wondered to himself if Mattie hadn't already lost him. She was thinking about losing him to a bullet. She could never conceive that he would leave her for another woman. He said, "I've got to go out now, Mattie. I'll be back as soon as I can. There is trouble in the streets."

Wyatt and Virgil and Morgan were standing on the boardwalk in the front of the jail. Before them, in the street, the cowboys were staging a parade, swaggering by defiantly, giving the Earps sidelong glances.

Meanwhile, the townspeople noticed and began to realize that something was about to happen.

Virgil said, "Here they are again. Look at them."

Wyatt said, "Easy, Virge, they are just trying to egg us on."

Virgil turned and moved into the jail. There was a vacant

lot behind the O.K. Corral, a popular stable that most of the cowboys used when they came to town. Beside the vacant lot was A. C. Fly's Photography Gallery on the left, and the Harwood house was on the right. The lot was about sixty yards across and forty yards deep.

The cowboys stood in a knot near their horses, passing a bottle around. Frank McLaury said, "I'd like to teach them bastards a lesson."

Billy Clanton said, "They probably already scared to death."

Tom McLaury said, "You called it, Ike. What are we gonna do?"

Ike grabbed the bottle and said, "Give me that. Dammit, I need some of this hair of the dog bad. My head is aching like hell."

He glanced up the street. He said, "I'd like to grind those damned Earps up into sausage meat and pass them around and feed them to the dogs. They've got theirs coming, make no mistake. I am tired of being shoved around by those Eastern punks. I don't see why we don't just take them. This is our town. They just come here. Why are we all just standing around? Let's go blow their damned heads off."

Virgil came out of the jail with a huge Stevens ten-gauge shotgun just as Doc appeared from around the corner.

Morgan said, "What're you doing out of bed, Doc?"

Doc said, "What the hell is going on? I've had ten people come up to me saying that the Clantons and McLaurys are comin' after me."

Wyatt said, "Don't worry, Doc, not your problem. You don't have to mix up in this."

Doc turned on Wyatt, genuinely shocked and hurt. He said, "That's a hell of a thing for you to say to me. How long we've been friends, Wyatt? How many fights have we made our own fights, you and me? Why should you say something like that to me?"

Wyatt was embarrassed. He tried to make up an excuse, saying, "Well, Doc, you weren't exactly lookin' your best, last night."

Doc returned, "Don't put me in my grave just yet, will ya, if you don't mind, my friend. I think I can hold up my end. That is, if you'll have me."

Wyatt said quickly, "Of course I'll have you, Doc. I don't know of another man I would rather have beside me 'sides you in a fight. I just meant that, you know, last night . . ."

Doc said, "Last night was last night. Today is today. Now, who are we gonna kill, and where is all the trouble?"

Morgan, trying to smooth the situation down said, "What the hell're we gonna do?"

Wyatt stepped down off the porch, took a few steps away from the O.K. Corral, and said, "Well, one thing we need to do is to wait till the liquor wears off. Once they start gettin' headaches, they'll lose interest. It's hard to make a gunfight with all that noise and a headache."

Doc said, "From the looks I've had of them, they're not trying to cure their headaches, they're trying to get more."

Virgil said seriously, "Wyatt, they're threatening our lives."

"Virge, you'll never make that stick."

"They're carrying guns in town."

Wyatt turned back and looked at Virgil. "They're carrying guns in town. Virge. That's a misdemeanor. You go down there to arrest 'em, something goes wrong, but maybe this time somebody gets his head broke. Suddenly it turns into a mess, and it won't end there. You'll have cowboys comin' around lookin' for trouble from here to Christmas. You gonna risk all that over a misdemeanor?"

Virgil paused, thinking the situation over, then said, "No, dammit, it's wrong. They're breaking the law."

Wyatt stopped and looked at him. He began to walk toward his brothers.

"All right, Virge, your call. But give Doc the shotgun. They'll be less apt to get nervy if they see him on the street with that howitzer."

Virgil handed Doc the shotgun and took Doc's cane. Doc folded it under his cloak. They were all set, waiting for Wyatt's cue.

Finally, he said, "Well, I don't like it, but I don't see much choice. Virgil, are you sure?"

Virgil said, "Yes."

"Well, come on, boys. Let's go see how things are at the O.K. Corral."

They started down Allen Street, their footsteps pounding on the board sidewalk. Virgil and Wyatt in the front and Doc and Morgan pulling up the rear. As they walked, bystanders stepped aside, trading whispers as they passed. The men turned onto Fourth Street.

They left the sidewalk and began walking down the middle of the road to avoid the crowd. As they passed they saw Turkey Jack Johnson and his friend Vermillion. Johnson called out and asked, "Can you use another gun?"

Virgil turned his head and shook it. He said, "Thanks, but I reckon this here is law work and we'd better handle it in the proper way."

Vermillion yelled, "Good luck."

They turned right on Freemont. Half a block away was the O.K. Corral. Morgan Earp could feel himself getting excited. All of his life, he had taken a backseat to his brothers, especially to Wyatt, and now he was going to have a chance to make a name for himself. Rather than being frightened, he was exuberant, thrilled at the prospect of having a gunfight. But then he was very young.

As if he knew what Morgan was thinking, Wyatt suddenly dropped back to walk beside him. He said, "Morgan, you remember what I said about how it feels to kill a man? I'm afraid you're about to find out. I just hope that you don't feel as bad as I've felt throughout the years."

Morgan said, "I don't see why it should feel bad if you're doin' the right thing and just defending yourself."

Wyatt shook his head and said, "Morgan, sometimes you just know that you are the better man, and you know the other man doesn't have a chance. But ya gotta go through with it, go ahead. On the surface, it looks like self-defense, but in your heart, you know it was still just murder."

All Morgan could do was look at him. He had heard the words, but he just couldn't quite understand them. He said, "If a man points a gun at me, I feel I have the right to stop him, and I'm gonna do it any way I can."

Wyatt shrugged. "Suit yourself." He quickened his pace and caught up with his older brother. For the first time he noticed the streaks of gray at Virgil's temples. He looked surprised. It seemed like yesterday, Virgil's hair had been the same color as his own.

The men were now coming into sight of the vacant lot and could see the horses standing near the back. The cowboys were standing, talking to one another as they watched the Earps walk closer toward them.

For Wyatt, apprehension had begun to set in. He wasn't afraid, just nervous. It was that high anxiety that he always got when he went into a dangerous situation.

He clenched and unclenched his fist several times, gritted his teeth, and his eyes darted back and forth. He counted the cowboys for perhaps the fourth time. There was still just the six of them: the two Clantons, the two McLaurys, Billy Claibourne, and Wes Fuller.

Almost unconsciously, all of the Earp party began to slow their pace as they crossed the street toward the edge of the vacant lot.

The cowboys moved forward in a line abreast. Ike Clanton was on one end, Wes Fuller was on the other. Billy Clanton stood next to Fuller.

From the way the cowboys were fidgeting, it was apparent that they were as nervous as the Earps. Only Doc Holliday seemed calm and complacent. He might as well have been on one of his afternoon strolls. At his side, he wore his .45 revolver and his .38 Colt Lightning Special was in his belt. The shotgun was still concealed beneath the large cloak he wore around his shoulders. He held it with his left hand. His cloak was shoved back with his right, revealing the handle of his .45 revolver.

The Earps and Doc Holliday came to the edge of the vacant lot and walked ten yards into it. They stopped.

Wyatt said to his older brother, "Virgil, you're making the arrest. I'll back you up and Morgan will back me up. Doc will keep his eye out for trouble. Keep your eyes on his gun. And keep yours hands on yours. If it even looks like something's gonna happen, buffalo them right off, right over their heads. Don't waste no time with birds like these. You can't trust them."

Virgil looked at Wyatt and said, "Wyatt, I know what I am doing. You're not the only lawman in this crowd."

He turned his head to look at the throng that had gathered across the street. He said, "Look at them all. They love it. Look at the vultures. Waiting for the dead meat. How the hell did we get ourselves into this?"

Wyatt said, "Because we're lawmen, we've always been

lawmen. Why don't you get that through your head. We'll always be lawmen, Virgil."

He was about to say more, but just then, John Behan came walking out of the shadows from A. C. Fly's Photography Gallery. He walked quickly up to Virgil. He said, "Virgil, you don't have to worry about a thing. I just went down there and disarmed them."

For a second Virgil's face lit up and then he said, "You did? Thanks. That's great." He almost sighed and turned to the others. "Well, come on, boys. Let's go on down there and round up our tame cows."

They passed under the hand-painted sign that announced the place as the O.K. Corral. They were within thirty yards of the cowboys when Wyatt suddenly stopped. He could plainly see that every one of the men was either armed or carrying a rifle. He said to Virgil, "Disarmed, my ass. Behan was trying to get us mowed down like new wheat. Every one of them suckers has got a gun. We better get ready for trouble and make no mistake."

Wyatt had his Ned Buntline Special stuck in his belt. Before he moved, he reached down and loosened it so that it would come out easily into his hand.

He glanced to his right. Morgan was wearing his gun holstered and he had his hand near the butt. Virgil had stepped just a little forward; his left hand was carrying Doc's gold-handled opera cane. He had thrown his cloak back so that his .45 revolver was clear to hand.

They moved forward slowly; each step seemed to take an eternity. As the distance closed from thirty yards down to twenty-five, Doc allowed the shotgun to slip out from his coat and into his hand. He carried it nonchalantly at his side, the barrel pointing not quite straight ahead.

Now they were in a line about four yards apart. They

were converging on the cowboys. Suddenly the legend seemed to come alive. No longer were they just four men walking on a vacant lot. They were four tall figures in long black coats, advancing in a line, grim and unstoppable.

A fleeting moment was frozen forever in time. Finally they did stop.

The cowboys had become increasingly jittery, even retreating a few steps. The two groups now stood about twenty feet apart.

Doc suddenly raised the shotgun. The Cheshire-cat smile spread over his face.

As the senior law officer, Virgil took two steps forward, his face set. He pointed the cane toward the line of cowboys.

He said, "We've come to arrest you. Throw up your arms."

There was a moment of confusion when nobody seemed to know what was going on or what was going to happen.

Suddenly Billy Clanton and Frank McLaury darted their hands toward their sidearms. The Earps instantly tensed up. Wyatt put his hand on the butt of his revolver. But Virgil waved his hands frantically, afraid they had misunderstood.

He said, "Hold it. I don't want that. We're here to arrest you, peacefully."

As if they had realized what was happening, Billy Claibourne and Wes Fuller suddenly bolted from the irresolute line and dashed toward Fly's Photography Gallery.

Everyone stopped. They stood still, both groups, staring after the two fleeing men. They watched, almost as if seeking a diversion, as first Fuller and then Claibourne almost dived into the backdoor of Fly's Gallery.

Then the two groups faced each other again. Wyatt Earp was watching Billy Clanton. Suddenly his eyes seemed to go dead and Wyatt groaned. He had seen that look before.

Now the time for all the name-calling was over. Now was the time for all the guns to speak. Wyatt knew what Billy Clanton was going to do almost before Billy himself did. He said, "Oh, my God."

It was Billy Clanton that he was most worried about. Suddenly Billy and Frank McLaury jerked their pistols and the scene began to explode as everything started to happen in a split second.

Wyatt drew in unison with Billy and Frank McLaury. He fired his first shot, knocking Frank McLaury down with a bullet in the gut.

Morgan fired, his shot driving Billy Clanton back against the hard wall of the Harwood house. Tom McLaury darted for cover behind his horse as Ike ran toward Wyatt, shrieking like a woman. He yelled, "Oh, no. Please, I don't have a gun." He came to within five feet of Wyatt.

Wyatt just looked at him and said, "This fight's commenced. Get to fightin' or get away."

Ike came close, clutching at Wyatt's arm. Wyatt hurled him aside. Ike suddenly turned and sprang toward the gallery.

Tom McLaury fired over his saddle at Doc, who tried for a shot but was blocked by the horse. Billy, who had been injured by Morgan's first shot, was backing up, screaming at the top of his lungs. He fired. The bullet took Virgil in the calf. Virgil sank, going to one knee, and then fell over completely.

Tom McLaury fired again, aiming at Virgil, and then he fired at Doc. Holding the shotgun down by his side, Doc fired one barrel into the air over the horse. The blast made the horse flare up, exposing Tom for a split second. In that second, Doc fired again, lower this time.

The shotgun shells caught Tom in the side, exploding his

flesh into a red mist as a full charge of buckshot slammed him back into the Harwood house.

Tom dropped his gun and teetered into the street, taking eerie little steps. He was already dead, but was still moving like a chicken with its head cut off.

Billy Clanton fired again. This time his aim hit home. He dropped Morgan with a hole in his shoulder.

On the ground, Morgan hollered out, "I'm hit."

Doc Holliday pulled his Lightning .38 double action and fired at Billy Clanton, hitting him in the abdomen. Frank was somehow back into the fight. He fired wildly.

Virgil was painfully getting himself back to his feet. He fired at Billy, but missed. The whole scene was now bathed in thick smoke as the fight started into the street, each man selecting his target.

Inside Fly's Photography Gallery, Billy Claibourne and Wes Fuller watched through the window as the fight progressed. Suddenly Ike came diving in. He snatched Fuller's pistol, smashed the window, and fired at Wyatt Earp.

Wyatt felt the bullet whiz by his ear. He knew it was coming from the wrong direction. He spun around, calling to Doc, "Watch out behind us."

In a flashing move that took less than a heartbeat, Doc pivoted, replacing the .38 in his right hand with his .45. With one pass of his left hand, with rapid fire quicker than you could count, he shot out four then five blasts.

The bullets ripped through the gallery, showering Ike and Wes and Billy with splinters of broken glass.

Fuller hauled Ike up and they all dashed toward the backdoor, Claibourne right behind them, all three frantically running for their lives.

Outside, Morgan Earp was still down. Virgil was now

erect, but it was plain that he was hurt and bleeding badly. He fired his revolver, but his shot was ineffective.

Only Wyatt Earp and Doc Holliday were shooting effectively.

Tom McLaury was dead, lying out in the street. Frank was hurt, but would not go down. The seemingly indestructible Billy Clanton had gotten to his knees. Holding his revolver with both hands, he steadied himself and fired.

Wyatt felt rather than saw the shot. Through the smoke haze, he could just make out Billy near the wall of the Harwood house. He aimed carefully, sighting down the long barrel and fired. The bullet hit Billy Clanton in the lower chest. Billy almost seemed to jump backward from the force of the slug. He hit the side of the house, bounced off, and fell on his face.

He was up almost immediately, trying to struggle to his feet. With a bloody hand, he clutched first at his hand and then at his wound.

In the middle of the lot, Frank McLaury suddenly staggered up. He bore down on Doc through the smoke. When he was five yards away, he said, "I got you now, you son of a bitch."

Doc almost laughed. He said, "If you do, you're a daisy. You're a real daisy."

In a gesture of contempt, Doc opened his arms and gave Frank a clear shot at his chest.

Frank stood there, swaying, brought his hand up with his pistol, and fired at Doc, the bullet going harmlessly wide. Frank took another step closer. He was about to fire again. But Doc said, "One free chance to a customer."

Doc Holliday's bullet had taken Frank McLaury straight through the heart, and in the next millisecond, he was lying on the ground, dead.

At almost the same time Doc fired, Morgan fired his big .45 from his prone position on the ground. The bullet hit Frank in the head as he was falling. As that last shot echoed through the hills Frank dropped limply to the ground like a rag doll with all the stuffing out of it, lying spread-eagle, finally no longer moving.

Billy Clanton leaned against the Harwood house, legs splayed out in front of him, absolutely shot to pieces, clicking his empty gun and wailing piteously as the smoke began to clear.

He said, "More cartridges. Somebody load my gun . . ."

As he said these words he sank to his knees and then slowly fell down on his face.

For a second it was very quiet and then the townspeople began to step timidly toward the site of the fight. A. C. Fly was the first one there. He ran to Billy's side, reached down, and took Billy's gun from his hand. The fight was finally, fatally, officially over.

For a few moments they all just stood there. Finally, Wyatt looked at Doc. Doc nodded. Then he turned his head toward Virgil. Virgil just gave his head a slight shake.

Then, as if they had been suddenly pulled, all three men rushed to where Morgan was struggling to sit up on the hard ground.

Wyatt said, "You hurt bad, brother?"

Morgan grimaced, holding his shoulder, and said, "Son of a bitch hit me in the joint, I think. Right in the shoulder joint. Hurts like hell."

Wyatt said to Doc, "We've gotta get these men to a doctor. Why ain't there a doctor here already? Is every doctor in this damned town deaf?"

John Behan came walking up and stood in front of the

little group, speaking in an official voice. "All right. You're all under arrest."

Wyatt looked up at him in utter disbelief. It took him a few moments to get the words out, such was his shock.

He said, "I don't think I'll let you arrest us today, Behan. Maybe tomorrow."

A large crowd had now gathered around the bloody lot around the O.K. Corral. From the back, the Earp women were trying to fight their way through.

Almost timidly, Josephine Marcus hung on the outskirts, trying to catch sight of Wyatt.

Allie and Lou forced their way through, with Mattie trailing them. They ran to Virgil and Morgan, hugging them.

Meanwhile, Doc Holliday stood over Frank's dead body. Looking down at him and jeering under his breath, he said, "You call that shooting?"

In the crowd behind them, Mattie had finally made her way to the front. She saw Wyatt, but Wyatt was not looking at her. Wyatt's eyes had found Josephine at the end of the crowd and their gaze stayed locked for a long moment. Mattie looked and saw the woman and then turned her gaze back to Wyatt. She needed no further answer. She turned and forced her way back through the crowd and walked down the street toward the little cottage that she had once called home.

Mayor Clum came up to Wyatt and said, "The McLaurys are both dead and Billy is just about the same."

Wyatt nodded and shoved his gun back into his waistband. He surveyed the bloody scene and said bitterly, "Well, I guess we've done our good deed for the day. Hope the folks enjoyed it. Should have charged admission. Of course, I reckon that killings are nothing new to this town, so I guess this was just all in a day's work, huh, Mayor?"

Chapter Eight

The cowboys were burying their dead and making quite a show of it. They marched the length of the main street, a little over fifty in all. Along the way, they threw fireworks into the crowd, shooting off Roman candles and skyrockets.

Their line of march took them straight toward Boot Hill. Curly Bill and Ringo right in the lead with Ike Clanton following behind. The three coffins and a banner that read MURDERED ON THE STREETS OF TOMBSTONE followed behind.

Wyatt stepped off the porch of his cottage as the cowboys marched past. He approached Curly Bill and said, "Curly, I am sorry. If there had been any other way . . . We gave them every chance."

Curly Bill said, "I know. You just did what you had to." He pointed toward the banner that was being carried, accusing the lawmen of being murderers, and said, "That banner stuff, that's just Ike. Don't worry about it."

Wyatt nodded, tipped his hat, and walked off.

Curly Bill looked at him walking away and whispered

softly, "Don't worry about a thing. Don't worry about a thing."

Wyatt stopped and stood by the side of the road watching as the cowboys continued their march up to Boot Hill. Then he turned and walked up on the porch. He sat down next to Morgan, who had his shoulder and arm in bandages. Wyatt had a hard time looking at his younger brother. Finally, he said, "Well, how you doin', boy?"

Morgan said, "Fine. Better."

Morgan looked tired and old, all the fun and youthful zest gone from his face. The sight that he couldn't get out of his mind was Frank McLaury's head exploding as that last shot of his took the already-dead man right through the temple. He could still see the spray of blood and bits of skull as the bullet exploded.

Morgan said, "You were right, what you said, you know, about killing a man. It was nothing like I thought. I almost wish . . ."

Wyatt said, "I know, kid. Me too." There was an unutterable sadness behind his eyes. This was the one thing that he had not wanted for his little brother. It had come to Virgil, and it had come to him, but he had hoped that it would never have to come to his little brother.

He had hoped it would have stopped with just the two of them.

The cowboys had gathered around a huge bonfire up in their roost at the end of the little valley in the hills. Sparks drifted up toward the heavens, and faces were vivid in the firelight, like an ancient gathering of warriors.

Curly Bill faced them, a bottle of whiskey in his hand. He said, "Here's to the memory of Billy Clanton and Tom and Frank McLaury. They went out real cowboys, dead game right up to their last kick. They won their places at the big table with Davy Crockett and Wild Bill and Old Man Clanton. They're up there right now tradin' shots with 'em. And they'll never be forgot. Not ever. Hundred years from now, there'll be settin' around a campfire just like this, telling stories about them boys. They're what you call immortal. And I say God bless 'em. Here's to them."

They all drank, long and deep. Even Ringo wiped away a tear, or at least pretended to.

Curly Bill said, "All right, I want everyone to listen to me." They all looked at him. "This whole thing's over. Nobody does a thing, ya hear me? Nobody does a thing."

The cowboys passed looks from one to another. They were in utter shock. Then Curly Bill smiled. It was an evil smile.

He said, "Until I say so."

Wyatt and Mattie were alone in their cottage. The parlor was a mess. Papers and litter were scattered everywhere. A chair was overturned. On the table, a bottle was on its side, slowly leaking soda water, which ran down the side of the table and made a pool on the floor.

Mattie sat in front of the empty hearth and slowly scratched her arms. There was a blank expression on her face as she stared into the empty fireplace.

In the other room, Wyatt had finished shaving. He stood there, wiping foam from his face. He opened the door of the cabinet to search for a towel, and when he did, a nest of small brown bottles clattered out and fell to the floor. They were laudanum bottles, all empty. He bent down and slowly picked up several of them, staring at them, frowning. He had known Mattie's habit had become worse, but he didn't know that it had gone this far.

He started toward the door and then hesitated. With Josephine on his mind, he especially didn't want to confront her. Mattie's sickness was like a barrier between him and the woman he really loved: the actress. The flashing, sophisticated lady of the stage. He somehow had to find a way to help.

But Mattie had to be dealt with.

Slowly he walked into the parlor, carrying three of the empty bottles. He waited until she turned around from her position in front of the fireplace. He said kindly, "Mattie, what about this? How come so many of these empty bottles? How far has this gone?"

Mattie looked sullen. She said, "I need it."

Wyatt sighed. "Well, at least you admit it."

"Admit what? That I need something to keep me warm at night. I'm not an opium fiend. I'm just a person who needs something, anything. A warm body. Someone to love me, someone to take care of me."

Wyatt said, "Look, Mattie, I know you are—"

Mattie cut him off. "No, Wyatt. You know nothing. Lord, it's when you're around that I need it the most. Sure, you smile sometimes, but there's no light in your smile for me anymore. Wyatt, there's nothing to keep me warm. I feel you in bed beside me and I know you are a hundred miles away, or at least a few blocks away." She paused. "A few blocks away to the hotel. Isn't that right, Wyatt? And I lay there, and I get so cold, Wyatt, I get so cold because you are not here. And you wonder about the opium. Why don't you just make it easier on yourself. Why don't you just say I'm an opium fiend and let it go at that. Don't take any blame yourself."

Wyatt said, "Mattie, now, look . . ."

She said, "No, you look, Wyatt. I want to know something. At least you owe me that much. I want to know what's between you and that actress woman."

Her words caught Wyatt off guard. He looked at her. She sneered back at him and said, "Is it a tough question, Wyatt? Is it hard to answer? Can't you think of an answer, Wyatt?"

Wyatt said, "All right, look. I can make it right. I can make this up to you, Mattie. I can, I swear. I swear I will do it. I will somehow get this thing straightened out."

Mattie suddenly stood up and faced him. Her face was flushed, whether from emotion or laudanum, it was hard to tell. She said, "Did you ever look at yourself, did you ever really look at yourself? You know that you worry more about those men that you killed than you do about me? You care more about the dead by your hands than you do the living. How can I compete with that? How can I compete with your conscience? How can I compete with that gun of yours? That horrible deadly gun that you swore that you would never use again."

Wyatt said, "Mattie, don't I—"

She cut him off again. She said, "You tell me to stop using laudanum and you swear that you'll never use a gun again. How long do your promises last, Wyatt? How long do your vows last?"

He stood there, his face suddenly pale. He could not speak. The images of the flashing guns, the smoke, and the red blood of the men on his hands. The falling bodies. It all flashed before his eyes.

He said, "Mattie, please, no. Don't talk to me like that."

Mattie said, "Now you know how I feel, Wyatt. Now you know how it feels to be empty inside. Now you know how it feels to not be able to trust yourself, to know that you can't control yourself. You can't control those guns any more than I can control the laudanum. And now you have gone to the bed of another woman."

Wyatt said, "Mattie, I don't want to—"

Again, she cut him off. She said, "Will you go there and tell her right in front of me that she's nothing to you? Right out loud so I can hear? Will you walk in there with me right beside you and tell her that she is nothing? Tell her that she's nobody, just dirt? Just a tramp? Will you do that?"

Wyatt stared silently at her.

She said, "Until you can do that, we've got nothing to talk about, Wyatt. Nothing. Now you just leave me the hell alone." She turned her back on him and started scratching her arms again.

For a moment Wyatt stood there, a stunned look on his face. Then, very slowly, he turned and started out the door. His mind was full, but he knew that somewhere inside of him was a void that nothing could fill, maybe not even Josephine. As he left he knew that he was leaving Mattie behind, maybe for good.

Wyatt and Doc Holliday sat at a round table in Doc's room in his boardinghouse. Kate wasn't there; it was just the two of them. There was a bottle of whiskey on the table in front of them.

Doc was sipping the whiskey slowly. He was already pleasantly tight. But Wyatt drank with the hard intensity of someone using the whiskey as some sort of an out, for some sort of relief.

Doc said pleasantly, "Wyatt, my boy, I don't know what's troubling you, but I will give you this sage advice of years of experience. Whiskey will not drown it, nor will it float it, nor will it wash it away. That, my friend, is something that you must do yourself. Whatever is troubling you, my boy, is not going away until you face it. Maybe it will never go away, even then." He laughed hollowly. "And I should know. Certainly I am a daisy of a one to know. There are many things that will never go away. You carry them like the heaviest loads on the back of a weak laborer. Always shouldering that load, waking up every morning with that load on your back."

Wyatt looked up at him. He said, "Doc, why do you always have to talk like that? Can't you just come right out and say something?"

"Ahhh, my boy, but it's so much more fun to disguise something from yourself. Like the lady up on the stage who disguised herself as Satan, but is a beautiful seductress."

Wyatt cut him off in a savage tone. "Doc, don't talk about her like that."

Doc said, "Ahhh, now perhaps we come to the crux of the problem. I didn't think that you had come to visit the old doctor just out of friendship."

Wyatt paused to pour himself another drink. With a set motion, he threw it back and set the glass on the table and took a moment to get a cigar from his pocket and light it. When it was drawing good, he said, "Doc, how are you feeling?"

Even though the ravages of the tuberculosis and the hard living were clear on his face and his frail frame, Doc smiled cynically. He said, "Just fine, Wyatt, mighty fine. Never felt better in my whole life. What's the old saying? In every way, every day, I get better and better."

For a moment Wyatt studied him. For some reason, he felt the answer to his own problem lay somewhere in the mind of the ravaged and suicidal man that sat across from him calmly pouring himself another drink. He asked, "Why don't you take better care of yourself? The doctors tell you, we tell you, everyone tells you. And yet you just go on trying to kill yourself. Can you tell me why?"

Doc laughed and said, "Son, you certainly are a fine one to talk. You ask me why I don't take better care of myself. Now I repeat the same question to you, sir."

Wyatt said, a little desperately, "I am not sick. I take care of myself."

Doc said, "Ah, but you are sick, Wyatt. You are the sickest of the sick. You are a man with a conscience who is forced by different elements, by lust, by honor, and by duty. The most deadly forms of disease. To do things that are against your conscience. Right now you sit before me suffering far worse than I. And we are only talking about one side of your life. There is another side that is even darker, even though it concerns the fairer sex."

He stopped talking and laughed, watching Wyatt over the rim of his silver shot cup.

Wyatt looked down miserably at his hands. He said, "Doc, I want to ask your advice."

"Oh, my boy, you are dipping your bucket in a poison well. My water is tainted. I bring death and war and pestilence and fire. My advice is to put a bullet through your brain and get it over with quickly rather than dragging it out forever. If that damned Frank McLaury could have shot a little straighter, I would have it over with and would not be sitting here now." He suddenly stopped as a fit of coughing racked him. For a second he bent double, a handkerchief to his lips. He coughed, seeming to bring up his lungs almost into his throat.

Wyatt hurried around the table and put his arms around the shoulder of his frail friend. "Doc, drink that whiskey down, quick, quick."

When the coughing slowed, Doc put the silver cup to his

lips and sucked at it greedily. Finally, as it settled, he gave a great shuddering gasp and then his breathing slowed.

He motioned Wyatt back around the table. "My son, look to your own ills. I'm fine, I'm fine. So how are we going to clear you of that conscience of yours? You didn't want to be a lawman, Wyatt. You quit because being a lawman involved hurting people, killing people. But you couldn't stay away from it. Is that what you want my advice about?"

Wyatt looked away. He said, "No."

Doc said, "I didn't think so. You're not content to be just a faro dealer. You're not content to have just one woman. You're not content to be happy. Wyatt, my boy, you're going to have to realize that there's a mark on some of us and that mark says disaster. You read it, you live it, and you know it in your heart and in your soul. No one else can see that mark because it's inside, but it spells unhappiness. Don't ever expect to be happy, Wyatt, because you never will."

"I don't want to believe that, Doc. I can't believe that." Wyatt's voice almost sounded desperate. "What do you do when you are in love with two women at the same time? 'Specially if one of them needs you more than the other, but you want the other one. What do you do then?"

Doc laughed. He said, "The oldest triangle of them all. I'll give you my heartfelt advice, but you won't take it, my lad. In later years, you will realize it's true. You will realize, never fall in love with anyone. There is no such thing as love, Wyatt. There is no such thing as good, there is no such thing bad. There is just life and then there is death. Accept that, and while you will not find happiness, you will find tranquillity that will ward off the torment during the long hours of the nights, and Wyatt, my nights are twenty-four hours long."

Wyatt stood up, pushing his chair back. He had a full glass of whiskey on the table in front of him. He took it down in one swallow and then slammed the glass back down on the table.

He said, "Doc, I care a great deal about you. You've been a great friend. But I hope to hell you are wrong about what you said."

Doc Holliday said softly, "So do I, my friend, for your sake, but I'm afraid I'm not." He raised his voice, saying, "Just remember, Wyatt, happiness rides a pale horse, my friend."

Wyatt asked, "Just what the hell does that mean?"

Doc said, "If you had read the Bible, you would know. Now, good day, my young friend, I intend to get drunk. Alone."

It was early evening. The Earp brothers came walking down the main street. Virgil was in the middle, flanked by Wyatt and Morgan. They were walking down the street to show themselves, but they were also checking the town. They wanted to make it clear to the townspeople that they had done nothing that they were ashamed of. They wanted to show the townspeople that they were there to protect them. They also wanted to show the cowboys that they weren't hiding.

Yet the townspeople seemed to avoid them as if they carried on an infectious disease, as if contact with them might suddenly cause the cowboys to choose them as targets.

Virgil said, "Getting a little warm. Spring is really here and summer will be comin'. This is going to be a beautiful country in the spring."

Morgan laughed and said, "Yeah, but come August, we might just wish we were back up north."

Billy Breakenridge walked into the middle of the street, stopped, and turned on them. He said, "It's Deputy Breakenridge. I don't wanna talk to you. Those men you killed were my friends. I'm just a nothing, but if I wasn't, I'd fight you. I'd fight you right now. So I don't wanna talk to you. You killed better men than you are."

He hurried away; the Earps watched him go in some amazement.

"Would you listen to that? All they ever did was make fun of him."

A voice suddenly sounded to their right. "Sister boy should've stuck around. I might have shown him something. He wanted to kill ya; maybe I'd've helped him."

They turned. A liquored-up Johnny Ringo stood behind them on the sidewalk like an apparition. There was murder in his eyes; his hands were thrust into the pockets of a short jacket. Ivory gun butts peeked out on both side.

Virgil said, "What do you want, Ringo?"

"I want your blood, I want your soul, and I want them both right now."

"For God's sake, Ringo, we don't want any more trouble. Now go on home."

Ringo stepped up to Wyatt and said, "Well, you've got trouble and it's gonna start right with you."

Wyatt said, "I'm not gonna fight you, Ringo. There's no money in it. You understand that? So sober up. Come on, Morgan, Virgil, let's move along. We've got a town to look after."

Wyatt turned into the Oriental Saloon; his brothers followed. Ringo howled after them. He said, "Wretched slugs, don't any of you have the guts to play for blood?"

There was another voice that sounded in the night. It came from just to Ringo's left.

It sounded deadly.

It said, "I'm your huckleberry. Come find me."

Ringo turned. Doc Holliday stood there, smiling that cat smile of his. Doc said, "Killing, that's just my game. Why don't you and I just play a few games?"

Ringo said, drunkenly, "All right, you damned lunger, have at it."

They faced each other, eyes blazing. In another second, the guns would be out and the fire would flash and the thunder of gunshots would sound.

Before that could happen, Curly Bill suddenly jumped between them with Stillwell behind him. They grabbed Ringo and pushed him away while the Earps grabbed Doc and pulled him away.

Curly Bill said, "Johnny, don't. Heavens. Come on, son." He turned and said, "Never mind him. He's drunk."

With an effort, they hauled Ringo up the street. When they got out of earshot, Ringo began cursing.

He said, "I want them spitting blood. I wanna gut-shot every one of them son of a bitches."

Curly Bill said, trying to calm him down, "Take it easy, Johnny, now ain't the time." He turned to the others. "I tell you what, boys, now I'm worried. What will happen when Ringo runs this outfit? Lord have mercy."

They pulled Ringo away from the doorway, away from the others. Ringo was so angry that he had tears in his eyes. He was clawing at the air. He said, "There is no God, there is no devil. I hate the whole damned world. I want to die."

His words echoed the earlier words of Doc Holliday. They came faintly to Wyatt Earp as he stood in the door of the Oriental Saloon watching the little drama playing itself out a short way down the street. It shocked him.

Curly Bill said, "Easy, son. Easy, Ringo. You just need to get your feet back under you, that's all. Gotta be patient, you understand?"

Ringo said, slurring his words, "I don't want to be patient."

Curly Bill said, "It will happen soon, I promise you."

His voice had dropped to a whisper as he said the last words.

Ringo also dropped his voice. "You mean it?"

Curly Bill answered, his voice still a whisper, "Yeah, I mean it. They'll never know what hit them. One at a time. *Bam-bam-bam*."

It seemed to mollify Ringo. He put his head down and half retched as if he was going to vomit, and then he pulled himself together. He said, "I need a drink. But let's not go into that saloon where that son of a bitch is."

The full nightfall, the wind howling down the street, kicking up dust in swirling columns. A flash of lightning streaked down from the purple sky; crashing sounds echoed through the town.

On the lighted porch of the Grand Hotel, Josephine Marcus sat reading a book. John Behan approached her. She looked up at his steps and bristled.

Behan said, "Listen, I want to talk to you."

"Not now. I don't have the time."

But Behan was insistent. "Listen, I saw that look pass between you and Wyatt at the fight. Listen to me. You're mine. Understand? You're my woman and I'm your man."

Josephine laughed. She said, "You told Wyatt you'd disarmed those men. Do you actually believe after that I could see you as my man? You're just a dirty little fixer. You're a liar. You are beneath contempt. Get away from me."

Behan's face was grim. He said, "Fine. You take it any way you want. I just wanted to tell you things are about to start changing around here."

"And what's that supposed to mean? And who is going to do the changing around here? A little old snake like you. I cannot believe that you told Wyatt that you disarmed those men. You could have gotten them all killed. You wear a badge, Mr. Behan, but you are not a sheriff."

Behan gritted his teeth. "So-called hard cases and tough nuts come and go around this town, but none of 'em's got a clue about a real play. None of 'em. After tonight, there's gonna be one guy in charge of Tombstone, and you'll be happy you know him. Bet on it."

She laughed. "It won't be you *Mister* Behan. The only thing that you will be in charge of is cowardice and lies and deceit."

His face went white. Then he whirled on his heel and walked rapidly away. She stared after him for a moment and then realized the meaning of his words. She got up, her face working, her mind going over the possibilities. She did not know what John Behan was up to, but she certainly knew that it boded no good for the Earps. To her, her duty was clear. She closed her book and went into the hotel to get her warp for the night air.

At Virgil's cottage, Allie and Louisa were sipping tea by a blazing fire in the hearth, warming themselves against the sudden storm's cold.

Allie said, "God, it's a cold night and just all of a sudden. Mattie, why don't you come up to the fire?"

Before she could move, there was a knock at the door. Outside, there was a tall silhouette of a woman in a dark cloak.

Louisa said, "It looks like a woman."

Allie crossed the room and opened the door. Josephine, breathless, entered the room. At the sight of her, Mattie sat up in shock. The others gathered around.

Josephine said, "Please, I know, it's awful me coming here, but listen, I can't say why, but I think something is—"

Before she could finish, there came a knock. Allie went to the window. She said, "There's another woman out there, almost in a cloak like yours, Josephine."

"I don't understand it."

Allie started to open the door, but Josephine suddenly leaped up and said, "No, look out." Then with her dancer's quickness, she dashed across the parlor, grabbing Allie and pulling her to the floor just as a tremendous shotgun blast ripped through the open doorway. The chandelier overhead exploded, showering the screaming woman with broken glass. A harsh male voice cut through the air as the shrouded figure dashed back into the darkness.

"Everybody dies," it cried, and then disappeared.

The women got up, shaking. Allie said, "My God, my God, somebody just tried to kill us." She turned to Josephine. "And he would have succeeded if it hadn't been for you. I'm in your debt."

Louisa said, "Who could it have been?"

Mattie said, "I don't know, but I think somebody better shut the door." She looked at Josephine as she said it.

In the Oriental Saloon, the sound of the shotgun blast was heard as Virgil got up from his seat and said, "Well, it's getting late, guess I'll turn in."

Wyatt said, "Bundle up, Virge, it's mighty cold out there."

He watched as Virgil left, making a little wave over his shoulder as he did. Wyatt and Morgan kept playing faro, hardly noticing as, moments later, Florentino walked out.

Outside, Virgil leaned against the wind and turned off Allen Street onto Fifth, his coattail whipping back and forth. He glanced up as Florentino walked by, crossed Fifth, and ducked into a doorway. Virgil stopped. Something seemed to be moving in the shadows of an unfinished building on the opposite side of Fifth.

Back in the saloon, Morgan and Wyatt heard a booming sound that echoed outside, partially muffled by the wind.

Morgan said, "That thunder's sure close."

Wyatt said, "That didn't sound like thunder."

Moments later Virgil walked back in, pale, hatless, a blank look on his face. He moved with odd, shuffling steps, holding himself sideways. Wyatt and Morgan exchanged puzzled glances.

Wyatt said, "Virgil."

Virgil said in an unsteady voice, "Wyatt . . . Wyatt . . . Wyatt . . ."

Virgil did a slight stutter step; his face took on a pleading, almost childlike look of panic. But as he turned his body toward Wyatt the younger Earp brother could see that Virgil's whole left side was in bloody shreds, and his left arm dangled unnaturally by a few gory ribbons of flesh. His voice was fighting sobs.

He said, "Wyatt . . ."

As he started to fall Wyatt rushed to him and grabbed him before he hit the floor. With Morgan's help, they eased him down.

Wyatt, his voice trembling, said to Morgan, "You better

run and get a doctor and you better do it quick. And if he don't want to come, you make him."

As Morgan rushed out of the Saloon Wyatt looked down at his now unconscious brother and said, "My God, how many doctors am I going to have to send for before I get out of this town?"

They carried Virgil to his cottage and laid him on his bed. The doctor attended him as Mattie and Wyatt watched. Allie was at Virgil's side, her hands over her mouth while the doctor worked over him with a sense of urgency.

Now, in the well-lit room, the severe damage that Virgil had sustained was evident. His left arm was in shreds. The blast had blown bits of cloth into his side and into his arm, which hung only by a few tendons. But in a way, he had been lucky. For if his left arm had not been where it was, his side would have taken the full blast of the shotgun and he would have died instantly.

As the doctor worked to cut away what was left of Virgil's coat and his shirt, he said, almost to himself, "Men do very strange things to each other. Why? Why? Why?"

Virgil gritted his teeth. At his side, Allie whimpered. Morgan and his wife were in the dining room, and in the background, they spoke in hushed tones. Morgan called to Wyatt.

Reluctantly, Wyatt left Virgil's side and moved into the dining room. As they began to talk Louisa excused herself and went into the parlor, where the shattered chandelier still bore witness to the earlier attack.

Morgan said, "Ya know they hit Mayor Clum's house too. They shot up his wife, Wyatt. His wife. Whoever heard of that? Men sneaking around in the dark, back-shooting, scaring women. Wyatt, they shot into this house, where your wife was, and my wife, and Virgil's wife. Even that actress

Josephine was here. Wyatt, they're scum. And all that small talk they made about live and let live. There ain't no live and let live with scum like that."

"Morgan, you've got to calm down. I know that you are upset. I'm upset too. I'm angry as hell. That is our brother lying in there shot all to hell. But you've got to listen to me. We gotta get out of here. We gotta put this behind us and get out of here before it's too late. Morgan, there is too many of them."

Morgan gave him a look of disgust. He said, "Listen to yourself, Wyatt. My God, you're Wyatt Earp. I've looked up to you all my life. Ever since I was aware of the man you are. And now you want to lie down and crawl away just because you may get hurt. Wyatt, what kind of talk is that?"

Wyatt looked down at the floor. He was torn. His best judgment told him there was nothing to be gained by the fight. He had to think of the others.

He said, "Morgan, use your head."

But Morgan wasn't hearing any of it. He pointed his finger toward the bedroom and said, "That's Virgil lying in there, Wyatt. Our own brother." His voice broke. "Why, he could be ruined for life. No, sir, I ain't going noplace. You want to go, fine. You go right ahead. You run if you want to. There's no run in me. And God help me, I never thought I'd see the day that there would be run in Wyatt Earp. But I'm staying right here and I'm gonna have it out with those bastards."

There was a sudden scream from the bedroom and then they heard Allie's voice saying, "What? What? No, no, you can't."

Wyatt and Morgan hurried into the parlor, where Louisa was holding Allie tightly to her chest.

The doctor turned to Wyatt. He said, "I'm afraid that your

brother has been very badly hurt. I'll have to remove the left arm at the elbow. What that means is, well, I'm afraid—"

Allie cut him off. She cried, "Oh no, no, no."

She started to wail. Suddenly alert, Virgil, the pain evident on his face, sat up. He reached out his big right arm and pulled her close. Somewhere he found the strength to reassure her. He said, "No, no, don't worry about old Virgil. He'll be all right. Don't take on so, sweetheart. Don't take on. You just make me feel worse."

She buried her face in his chest and sobbed. For a moment he held her and rocked her back and forth. Morgan, in the doorway, turned; he was about to leave. The anger and pain was clear on his face.

Wyatt whipped his head around. He said, "Morgan, wait." He turned back to Virgil and said, "Virgil . . ."

Allie looked at him, her eyes dancing with fire. She said, "You had to be so damned smart. Wyatt Earp."

Wyatt said, "I'm sorry I told you—"

Morgan cut him off. He said, "Wyatt, I don't think any of us should talk right now."

Wyatt's face was full of misery. He said, "Virgil, what do you want me to do?"

Virgil looked away. He said, "For God's sake, just leave me alone. Haven't you done enough already?"

Wyatt backed away. He turned and looked pleadingly at Mattie. She looked away. He slowly turned on his heel and walked out of the cottage door. His heart, his mind, his soul, and his spirit were at the lowest ebb he could remember in his life. It seemed to him that he had gone against everything he had ever believed in. He had gone against his own conscience, he had gone against his own courage. He had gone against Wyatt Earp.

Doc's words came back to him. Now they haunted him

like a familiar old refrain. He was a man with too much conscience for the job that was at hand. Well, he thought, maybe something could be done about that.

As he walked out in the street he froze as he saw Frank McMasters approaching with Turkey Creek Johnson and Jack Vermillion in tow. He put his hand to the butt of the revolver that was still in his holster.

McMasters said, "Hold it right there, Wyatt. I'm not here for trouble. Just the opposite. Listen, I know that nothing I can say will fix things, but I want you to know that it wasn't me."

Wyatt sneered at him. "No, I thought you brothers were brothers to the bone, right?"

"Not anymore. Not after this." McMasters's voice was sad. He looked down at the ground and then looked up at Wyatt and said, "I don't belong to them anymore. I'm not part of that crowd anymore."

While Wyatt watched he slowly untied the red sash around his waist and let it drop to the ground. Then, for good measure, he ground his heel into it.

Wyatt looked down at the sash and then up to McMasters's eyes. He could see the conviction in the man.

Turkey Johnson said, "He means it, Wyatt. If you need us for anything, we're here. Whatever, you name it, we're ready."

And then in the stillness of the night, there came the sudden sound of gunshots ringing out. They went *Blam. Blam. Blam.*

Wyatt's head snapped toward the sound. The shots came from the direction of the Oriental Saloon. With the help of Turkey Johnson and Frank McMasters, he shouldered his way through the crowd that had gathered outside the saloon.

Inside, his eyes went immediately to Morgan, who had

been laid out on the pool table. His shirt had been pulled up; his chest was covered in blood, some of it leaking off and staining the green felt of the pool table. In a corner, a stray dog had taken refuge. He lay there moaning as if it had been him that had been shot.

Wyatt rushed to Morgan's side. He could see that the wound was awful, a bullet through the chest.

Morgan looked up at him. He licked his lips, wanting to say something.

Wyatt said, "Morgan, just take it easy, please. The doctor is coming. He has been sent for. He's just finishing up, he's finished with Virgil, he'll be here any minute. Just hang on, please."

Hoarsely, Morgan said, "You gotta watch out, Wyatt. They're . . . they're . . . they're kill crazy. You watch out. Watch out for us all, Wyatt. You . . . you . . . you—"

Wyatt put his hand over his brother's mouth. He said, "Please, Morgan, don't try to talk right now. Save your strength. Save all the strength you've got."

The doctor came elbowing through the crowd, his shirt still stained with Virgil's blood. He came up to the table, opening his bag, and took out a bullet probe. He said to Wyatt and Johnson and to McMasters, "You're gonna have to hold him. This is gonna hurt."

The three of them took Morgan by the arms and shoulders as the doctor began to probe. Morgan jerked violently. Suddenly he let out a gritted scream. He was joined by a much louder one. It came from Louisa as she burst through the doorway, tearing her hair, in utter hysterics.

Wyatt looked up. He said, "Oh no, not now, Lou. Get her out of here, please. Please, get her out of here."

The scene was one of hellish confusion, with the dog

whimpering, Louisa shrieking as others tried to hold her, and Morgan on the table wailing as the doctor probed.

Suddenly Morgan gave a violent jerk, almost breaking loose from the grip of the three men. He snarled, almost at the end of his rope.

The doctor said, "Hold him, dammit, hold him. How many of your Earps am I gonna have to work on before this is all over with? I said hold him."

The dog howled louder, but by now, the friendly hands had taken Louisa out the door so she could no longer hear her husband's cries.

Wyatt yelled, "Somebody shut that damned dog up."

From his place on the pool table, Morgan took Wyatt's arm and spoke. His voice was like a child. He said, "You were right, Wyatt. They got me good. Don't let them get you too."

Wyatt was almost in tears. He said, "Will somebody get that damned dog out of here?"

Morgan said, "Remember about the light you're supposed to see when you're dying?"

"Easy, Morgan, don't think about that right now."

"It isn't true. I can't see a damned thing. It just keeps getting blacker and blacker and blacker. Wyatt, Wyatt, are you still there? Wyatt?"

Tears were welling up in Wyatt's eyes. He said, "I'm right here."

He took Morgan's hand and squeezed it.

Morgan said, "Wyatt, it's so black. . . ."

Then he opened up his mouth to speak again, but no sound came out. His lips slowly closed, but his eyes stayed open, staring at the ceiling. In disgust, the doctor hurled his probe across the saloon.

Wyatt said, "Morgan, Morgan, Morgan . . ." But it was no use. He shook his brother.

The dog started howling louder and longer, and in the next moment the air was filled with howls as every dog and coyote for miles joined in the mourning.

Slowly, Wyatt backed away from his dead brother.

He turned, and for a moment he stared at the crowd that was still gathered around the door. They shrank from the look in his eyes.

Not seeming to see where he was going, Wyatt walked through the crowd that parted as he came. McMasters and Johnson and Vermillion followed him at a distance. Wyatt stopped out in the street and looked at the blood on his hands. His brothers' blood, both brothers. They were commingled now. There was the blood in his veins and the blood of Virgil on his hands and the blood of Morgan on his hands.

He stood there, just off the boardwalk, near the center of the street.

Then Josephine saw Wyatt and started running to him.

Wyatt looked up and saw her coming toward him. Then he looked around at the crowd. He saw his wife, Mattie, but more than that, he saw red sashes in the crowd watching.

As Josephine faltered she said, "Wyatt."

Wyatt said, "Go away, don't come near me. I don't want you near me."

But she would not stop. Finally, she was in front of him. She started to put her hands to his face.

In desperation, Wyatt took her by the shoulders and pushed her away. Only her dancer's balance kept her from falling.

He said, "You whore, you filthy whore. Get away from me. Run to John Behan. Just get away from me."

She stared, unable to believe her ears. For a second, her face was a mask of confusion. Then she ran swiftly away.

A few feet away, Doc and Kate had witnessed the scene between Josephine and Wyatt. Fuming with rage, Kate started toward Wyatt, but Doc pulled her back.

She said, "That son of a bitch. Did you see that?"

Doc cut her off. "Woman, are you so dense that you can't see that he had to do it. He had to do it for her sake. I know that you probably can't understand that, but you just witnessed a noble act. You may not have sense enough to know that."

Together, Doc and Kate stared after Wyatt. He was walking down the middle of the street. The dogs were still howling as Wyatt stumbled in a daze.

Suddenly he doubled over, clutching his abdomen in agony. The agony of his lost brother.

The wagon bearing Morgan's pine coffin waited in the street, hitched and ready. Virgil waited up front with the women, his arm in a sling. His face pale. Doc Holliday and Kate waited on horses nearby. Only a day had passed since Morgan's death, but it seemed like an eternity, so changed had the town become.

The loading was finished. They were waiting for nothing but Wyatt. He had gone into the telegraph office without telling anyone the reason. People lined the street and watched in silence.

Mayor Clum and his wounded wife stood and watched from the window of their lodgings next door. They were not able to go outside and meet the gazes of the Earp survivors.

The very air was charged with paranoia and recrimination as if the whole town had suddenly become ashamed of itself.

In front of the hotel, Josephine Marcus stood and looked on. She was looking for Wyatt, wondering where he could be. She felt that she had to speak to him at least one last time.

Then Wyatt came out of the telegraph office and walked straight past her, without a word, without so much as a look.

Curly Bill watched. He said, "Look at that, he cut her dead. Now she's nobody. We can just leave her alone. Wyatt just dumped her. He wouldn't care what happened to her."

Doc Holliday saw the same scene, but he knew the correctness of the matter. He said, "And so she walked out of our lives forever." His tone was sarcastic.

Without saying a word to anyone, Wyatt climbed into the seat of the wagon and took hold of the reins. He gave the horse a slap and began to drive off slowly.

But then he stopped, pulling up in front of the cowboys. They made a show of hiding their weapons. Wyatt looked straight ahead, not looking at them.

He said, "I want you to know that it's over and we're not coming back."

Curly Bill said, "Well, 'bye. Been nice knowin' ya."

Ringo made a show of sniffing something in the air. He said, "Hey, you smell that? Smells like something died around here."

Curly stifled a laugh. He said, "Oh hell, Johnny."

Allie's eyes flared and Louisa stifled a sob. The cowboys snickered. From across the street, Frank McMasters looked at them as if to memorize everything about them.

Wyatt clenched his teeth, still staring straight ahead. He slapped the horses again and drove on.

When they were a hundred yards away, Curly Bill turned to Ike and said, "I want you to take Frank Stillwell and finish it."

But Ike was staring across the street at Frank McMasters. He said, "What's that all about with Frank McMasters? He ain't wearing his sash."

Curly Bill said, "Don't worry about it. I'll take care of it later."

The wagon creaked slowly out of town, taking the road to Gayleyville, which was the nearest railroad terminus. It would be a hard day's drive, a sad day's drive. The Earps were leaving Tombstone with one of them dead and the other two brothers who would never again be the same. Virgil from the loss of his arm and Wyatt from the loss of something much more valuable to him.

The telegraph Wyatt had sent had been to the United States Marshal Crawley Dake. He expected to meet Dake in Gayleyville.

Out behind the hotel, Doc saddled his horse. Kate stood by, her face a mass of frustration and helplessness. A resolute Doc Holliday rammed his rifle into his saddle boot as Kate began to plead, almost beside herself.

She said, "It's Wyatt, isn't it? You're going with him, aren't you? Why don't you stay with me?"

Without looking around, Doc said, "I can't."

"I don't understand. I'm your woman. I've always been your woman. Where does this leave me?"

Doc laughed. "Without a meal ticket, I suppose. But don't worry, you'll find another poor soul in need of your services, my dear."

Now Kate was angry. She said, "You bastard. Oh, you're a bastard, Doc. And after what all I've done for you."

He turned to face her. "I'm leaving now, dear." His voice became sincere. "Have you no kind word for me before I ride away? Just one?"

A genuine warmth was in his face, but she turned angrily away. He shrugged, reflecting that it was pointless for a man to show his true feelings. He said, "Well, I calculate not."

Then he put the spurs to his horse and galloped off without looking back.

Chapter Nine

Two porters loaded Morgan's coffin into a boxcar at the Gayleyville train station. Up ahead, Mattie and Louisa fumbled with their luggage while Allie boosted Virgil up into a passenger car.

The conductor walked slowly down the mixed train of passenger and freight cars. He yelled, "Board. All board. Board. All aboard."

From the shadows beside the depot, Ike Clanton and Frank Stillwell suddenly emerged. They both were carrying shotguns. They crouched, looking at each other and exchanging nods, and started forward, cocking their weapons. They had to squint as a blast of steam came boiling from the engine.

Stillwell said, "That's Virgil with the women. But where the hell's Wyatt?"

Ike looked around nervously and said, "I don't know. Ain't he on the train?"

"He can't have been. We been watching all this time. Where the hell can he be?"

From behind them, Wyatt's voice sounded. "I'm right behind you Stillwell."

The two gunmen spun around. Wyatt stood there. Ike and Stillwell were looking down the barrel of Virgil's big ten-gauge shotgun.

Frantically, Frank Stillwell tried to raise his own shotgun, but he never got the chance, he never got it horizontal. Wyatt fired and Stillwell was knocked backward like a rag doll. He hit the floor in a crumpled heap, his torso a smoking bundle of bloody rags.

From all around, there were screams and reactions from the startled bystanders. They began to panic, but Marshal Crawley Dake quickly stepped out and showed them his badge. He pushed the crowd back. He turned and nodded toward Wyatt.

Wyatt stepped toward Ike Clanton. Ike immediately dropped his shotgun and fell to his knees in terror as Wyatt turned the other barrel of his shotgun on him.

Ike spoke, trembling. "Oh, please God. Please, please. Wyatt, I never done anything to you."

Without taking his eyes off the quivering Ike Clanton, Wyatt shouted at the conductor, "Get this train out of here."

As the train pulled out, Virgil craned his neck out the window. Wyatt looked at him and raised one finger. The meaning was clear. The first one had gone down. Virgil smiled and nodded.

With Clanton still on his knees before the shotgun, four figures appeared through the steam. There was Doc Holliday, Jack Vermillion, Turkey Johnson, and Frank McMasters.

Wyatt turned back to Clanton and opened his coat. He said, "Take a look at this, Ike. Take a real good look. This ain't no town marshal's badge I'm showing you. This ain't no sheriff's badge. Take a good look. What does it look like, Ike?"

Ike said, his voice trembling, "Why . . . why . . . it's a U.S. marshal's badge. Are you a U.S. marshal, Wyatt?"

"You're right, Ike. You called it. You also called down the thunder on you and the rest of them like you. Well, now you're gonna get it."

He walked over and kicked Ike to his feet. Ike scrambled up and stood there shaking, he was so frightened.

Wyatt said, "Ike, I'm not gonna kill ya. Not right now. And for one reason and for one reason only. I want you to carry a word back to your bunch that style themselves as the cowboys, all those gentlemen who wear the red sashes. You tell them that Marshal—United States Marshal Wyatt Earp is coming for them. You tell them that they'd better keep watch. You tell them that every time they look over their shoulder, they'll see me or one of my men. You tell them that every time they look to the side, they'll see me or one of my men. You tell them my best advice is to get out of the country or get ready to get buried."

Ike needed no further invitation. He turned and went racing down the platform, jumping off the end and disappearing into the darkness. His shotgun lay right where he had left it.

Wyatt laughed and picked the shotgun up. He said, "You run, you cur. Run and tell all the other curs. Tell 'em I'm comin' to southeast Arizona . . . and hell is coming with me, you hear? *Hell is coming with me.*"

Out under the hot desert sun, Wyatt sat on his horse, his right hand uplifted. In front of him, four men stood. Doc Holliday, Turkey Johnson, Jack Vermillion, and Frank McMasters.

Wyatt said, "Do you solemnly swear to uphold the laws and constitution of the United States of America and to protect her citizens to the best of your ability, even at the cost of your own life?"

One by one they said, "I do."

Wyatt lowered his hand. "You are now duly authorized deputy United States marshals." He smiled and said, "That was the easy part. Now let's get to work."

Without saying another word, they all jumped into their saddles and began to ride southeast toward Tombstone. Toward the home of the cowboys. No one was smiling.

Near a saloon on the outskirts of Tombstone, a place that was frequented by the cowboys, a half dozen of the outlaws sat around, drinking, laughing, and talking about what they had done to the Earps.

Suddenly glasses began to rattle. One of the cowboys said that something was about to happen. And suddenly it did.

A horse came crashing through the big plate-glass window. It was Wyatt. His horse landed in the middle of the saloon in the shower of broken glass. His long revolver was already in his hand and pointed toward the cowboy's face.

He said, "I'm a United States marshal. Reach."

At that instant, Johnson, McMasters, and Vermillion came walking through the front door. They spread out, holding guns on the outlaws.

Behind the bar, the bartender fell to the floor. In the saloon, others who were wearing red sashes, dropped down, covering their heads. Only the cowboys stood up, looking wildly back and forth.

Johnson yelled, "Nobody moves."

But just then, Doc Holliday came sauntering in the backseat and said, "Nonsense, by all means, move."

He smiled. Across the room, a nervous cowboy reached for his gun. He never reached the butt as Doc Holliday blew him almost in half with a shotgun blast. It was the signal for the start of the battle.

Within thirty seconds, seven more of the cowboys lay dead on the floor. With the exception of a bullet graze on Turkey Johnson's face, none of the marshals had been harmed.

Before he left, Wyatt turned to the shaken bartender. He was still astride his horse. "You better tell any of the rest of your patrons that come in here wearing the red sashes, it's a good way to get killed."

With that, he rode his horse out the front door to where the others were waiting.

Johnson and Vermillion were laughing. Wyatt rode up and said, "A little too early to start celebrating, boys."

Turkey Johnson looked up at him and said, "Yeah, but wasn't it fun?"

Wyatt's face was grim. He said, "When it's all over, then it will be fun. We got a long way to go. That's only eight of them down. Mount up, we've got a long way to go."

It was almost dusk at the little plain atop the line of purple hills where the cowboys made their main camp. About two dozen of them were there, some cooking, some tending to their horses. Pony Deal, the half-breed, and four others were engaged in a game of poker. Behind Pony Deal and the poker game was the corral where the cowboys kept their horses.

Off farther to one side, a number of pens were filled with stolen cattle.

At the camp, four of the cowboys sat around cooking pieces of meat on long branches of green wood. Back over near the poker game, watching aimlessly, Floren Florentino seemed to be all by himself. He was deep in thought about the reports he had heard about what Wyatt Earp and his four deputies had done so far. He had good reason to be troubled. He suspected that Wyatt knew that it was he who had shot Morgan.

Of course, he was only one of several who shot Morgan, but he had heard rumors that Wyatt had singled him out particularly.

There was a distant sound, almost like the noise of someone drumming his fingers lightly on a table. As the moments passed, it grew louder. The cattle in the pens became restless. Now and then, one of them made a lowing sound. The four cowboys around the campfire looked at each other apprehensively.

The sound was coming louder and louder. Almost at the same time they recognized it as the sound of hooves, the sound of many hooves. Then there was a sound like crashing thunder as the five horsemen came flying over the ridge and onto the plain.

The four startled cowboys at the campfire jumped. It was a mistake, because Wyatt and his four deputies drove their horses straight through them, knocking them down like so many cords of wood.

As they crashed through them and passed on by, Doc Holliday who was riding up the rear, turned and fired both barrels of his double-barrel shotgun into the four men. Three went down instantly, and one staggered away, his hands clamped to his bleeding face.

Wyatt swung his men in a semicircle, heading for the center of the camp. They fired indiscriminately as the cowboys started to run. Wyatt jerked his big black horse to a stuttering halt and leaped from the saddle. In his left hand, he held the quirt, and in his right, his long .45 Peacemaker.

Without pause, he yelled as his deputies dismounted. He said, "You're all under arrest. Throw down your arms and put your hands up in the air. Next man to move dies."

For a second the cowboys were stunned, but one looked around and calculated the number of them compared with the number of deputies. Emboldened by their superiority in numbers, he stepped toward Wyatt Earp.

He said, "Who the hell do you think you are, Wyatt Earp? We run you once and we'll run you again. And if you have any more brothers you want killed, why, bring 'em—"

He got no further as Wyatt slashed him across the face with his quirt, cutting him to the bone. In the same motion, Wyatt shot the man point-blank in the chest. The cowboy fell backward as if hit by a giant fist.

The rest of the cowboys stayed just exactly as they were. None of them dared to move under the menacing guns of Wyatt Earp and his deputies. They stood, stock-still, frightened.

Wyatt let his eyes roam over the remaining men.

A worried-looking Florentino was trying to hide behind two men as Wyatt started to step in his direction. Florentino suddenly bolted and started running. He was twenty yards away, heading toward the remuda and his horse in the corral.

With a single move, Wyatt leaped on his horse and laid on the spurs. The horse closed the distance within seconds. Florentino glanced back and tried to run faster, pulling a belly gun from his sash as he did. Wyatt was almost on top of him. Florentino turned and fired on Wyatt; the bullet went wild. Wyatt kept going, drawing his Buntline, impervious, unstoppable.

Florentino turned for another shot just as the black

stallion piled into him and sent him tumbling down an embankment.

He scrambled to his feet as Wyatt dismounted. Wyatt started toward him with a deliberate step, eyes blazing, the long-barreled pistol held in front of him.

Shaking his head, Florentino backed up in terror, the gun at his side. Wyatt nodded, still stepping slowly.

There was cold-blooded murder in his eyes.

Florentino screamed and started to raise his gun. At that moment Wyatt fired, blasting Florentino to the ground. He advanced, firing again and again. He fired until the hammer clicked on an empty cylinder.

He looked down at Florentino, who was literally shot to pieces, and said, "That's for Morgan. He sends his best."

Pony Deal and ten of the cowboys had just made a cattle raid into Mexico. Now, in the late afternoon, back in Arizona, after driving the cattle from Mexico, they neared the roost. They still had ahead of them another low line of the hills that dot the barren Arizona plain.

They could have driven around them, but the cattle were weak. There was a water hole just on the other side of the hills. There was also a cut through the hills, and Pony Deal had decided that they would take this shortcut.

They drove the seventy or eighty cattle ahead of them toward the cut. As they neared, the lead rider suddenly threw up his hands to stop the party. He pointed. Pony Deal rode toward the front. He was amazed to see several horsemen positioned in the mouth of the cut. He felt his heart beat a little faster.

He couldn't be sure, but something told him it was Wyatt Earp and his four deputies. He looked around. Did it make a difference? he thought to himself. They outnumbered the deputies two to one. Maybe, he thought in his half-breed heart, this was his chance to finish off that damn Earp, that turncoat McMasters, and the rest of the deputy marshals.

He said to one of the cowboys, "Let's push these cattle fast. Let's push them right toward them son of a bitches."

The cowboys started forward, forcing the cattle to a trot. As they neared, Pony Deal could definitely tell from the black horse and the way the deputies were spread around him that it was indeed Earp.

He urged his men to quicken the pace. They started to charge, leaving the cattle behind them. When they were only a hundred yards away, he thought they had them. He drew his revolver and began to yell wild curses into the air.

As they came closer Pony Deal readied himself to fire. Then suddenly Wyatt Earp and his men turned and headed into the cut. The cowboys kept their horses running at top speed.

Wyatt's group reached the little trail that he had used before that led up the wall in the cut. Unseen, they clambered up the side at a bounding gallop, and a few moments later the cowboys galloped by and continued through to the desert on the other side, leaving their cattle behind.

Wyatt and the deputies careened up and around the high mountain wall as if on a roller coaster. They followed the tiny, narrow path at a breathtaking clip. The trail finally plunged them back into the draw behind the cowboys.

They sped up to the opposite mouth of the cut, at the end of the little row of hills. They drew their pistols as the cowboys rode in front of them, completely unaware.

In a line, abreast, Wyatt and his men charged. The cowboys, seeing no one in the desert ahead of them, pulled up in confusion. Suddenly there was a volley of gunshots behind them. Some of them were hit, knocking them from their saddles. The rest spun around just as Wyatt's group slammed into them head-on, guns blazing. The cowboys tumbled from their saddles left and right, and horses reared and toppled over backward.

It was a scene of mass confusion.

Realizing their plight, the remaining cowboys turned and tried to dash into the desert.

Wyatt shouted, "Let's get them, boys." Wyatt and his men charged. In a few bounds, they had caught the fleeing outlaws. Jack Vermillion stood in his stirrups, roaring like a wild animal, as he plunged into them. He swung his quirt like a saber and lashed a cowboy across the face. The blow made the cowboy tumble to the earth and bounce over the rocks.

Frank McMasters closed down on another, putting his arm around him and jerking him from his saddle, snapping his neck.

As Doc Holliday overtook a third cowboy he jammed his pistol into the man's face and fired point-blank, blackening his face with soot and blowing out the back of his head as he fell.

Reins in his teeth, shotgun at his shoulder, Johnson came up behind a fourth and fired. The cowboy's head disappeared in a cloud of pink vapor, the body dropped like a stone.

Pony Deal was fleeing at a dead run, but behind him, Wyatt was closing in on him on the back of his magnificent black stallion. As he came near, Wyatt swung out of his saddle like a Comanche and ducked his body down against the side of the horse, hiding in its bulk.

Pony Deal turned and looked back, his gun ready for a shot. All he saw was an apparently riderless horse overtaking him. But in the next instant, Wyatt rose back into the saddle and fired, blowing Pony Deal head over heels off the back of his horse.

Ahead, Wyatt could see Frank McMasters riding hard after a young cowboy, the lone survivor. Wyatt started his horse into a run, trying to catch McMasters as the deputy lifted his rifle, drawing a bead on the young cowboy.

It was Ward, Bob Ward. A young man new to the brand.

He was only a few yards in front of McMasters now. He whipped his horse frantically, trying for more speed.

McMasters was about to fire when Wyatt rode by, deflecting the shot. The young cowboy made it over the rise and disappeared. McMasters looked around at Wyatt in surprise.

He said, "What'd ya do that for?"

Wyatt said grimly, "So he can tell the story. I want word to get back to Curly Bill that he's next."

Crouched down low in the dirt, Curly Bill studied a map that had been drawn at his feet with a stick.

Bob Ward turned to him. "Didn't make any sense. One minute we're chasin' 'em, the next they're right on top of us. They got everybody, just everybody!"

"Easy now; you're young and scared," Curly Bill said. "But its only five men. They've been hittin' the waterholes and that Judas McMasters is showin' 'em. But I got an idea bettern any they had so far," he continued, pointing down to the map.

"What do you mean?" asked Ward. He still sounded spooked.

"Iron Springs," Curly Bill said solemnly. "That's where they show next. Only we're gonna be there first. And throw us a little party." He grinned, his coarse face ghastly in the firelight.

Near a water hole, two cowboys crouched by a fire while they sipped coffee. Behind them, Wyatt and his men rode quietly to an outcrop of rocks overlooking a spring and dismounted unseen.

McMasters said, "They are here. No herd, though."

Wyatt said, "We'll go around that yonder way and come up on foot."

They pulled shotguns from their saddles and started down the rocks on foot, creeping up on the camp, seemingly undetected. But, unexpectedly, the cowboys dived behind a log.

McMasters yelled, "Ambush. Get down."

They fell to the ground, as if dead, as the opposite side exploded into gunfire. Vermillion took a graze and dropped with the others, hugging the rocks. A bullet ricocheted into a rock at Johnson's head, biting his face with fragments. It made him wince.

Johnson said, "Holy hell."

Hunched down behind the logs on the opposite side were fifteen more cowboys. Curly Bill raised his head. He grinned and shouted, "Hey, Wyatt. How the hell are ya?"

Wyatt and his men did not react to his voice. The fire continued. Suddenly there was movement on the rocks above them. Doc pointed and said, "Wyatt, look."

Curly Bill yelled, "Got some boys workin' around those rocks behind you. Another minute or two, gonna have you in a cross fire. How do ya like that?"

McMasters saw the spot they were in. He said, "He's right. They get set up in the rocks, it's the end for us."

For the first time there seemed to be fear in these men.

Curly Bill laughed again, his voice booming out in the night. He was having the time of his life.

He said, "Of course, you could give yourself up and we could have us some kinda party. Them would be just some kind of skylarks, wouldn't they?"

Crouched by Curly Bill, a cowboy chuckled. A confident ripple of laughter ran through the cowboy line.

On the other side of the rock, Vermillion shook his head vehemently.

He said, "They ain't taking me alive, dammit."

McMasters looked at the still-silent Wyatt. He shrugged helplessly.

McMasters said, "Think of something fast or we're cooked."

They felt that they were running at the end of their rope. They all looked to Wyatt for the answers. He remained silent. Then, in this supreme moment, a strange, almost supernatural calm seemed to come over him and he said simply, "No."

Turkey Johnson said, "What?"

Wyatt said, "No."

The others stared at the strange look on Wyatt's face and then looked on in horror as he rose to his feet, exposing himself.

Doc yelled, "Wyatt."

Bullets began to whiz around him. Doc jumped up to grab him, but a ricochet drove him back down. Wyatt advanced quickly across the clearing. He was walking right into the teeth of their guns.

As he walked he repeated, "No."

His clothes jerked and ripped as the bullets passed through, but he just kept going.

Seeing this, Curly Bill also stood up. A weird, manic elation came over him. He hooted and howled.

Curly Bill said, "Yeah, look at that. Yeah, come and get some, boy."

Wyatt said, "No . . ."

Curly Bill waved away his men's fire and walked toward Wyatt, his twelve-gauge shotgun in one hand and his .45 in the other. He started firing when he was fifteen yards away.

Curly Bill said, "Let me, let me, yeah. Die you bastard."

Wyatt said, "No . . ."

Curly Bill fired again. Wyatt's hat flew off. Curly Bill fired again, digging a gash in Wyatt's boot heel. Now Curly Bill fired his .45 again and clicked. He fired on empty. He tossed it aside.

Suddenly a sharp wind gusted up, making the tails of Wyatt's duster swirl around his legs as he advanced. His eyes wild with rage, Curly Bill yelled, "Now you will die, you son of bitch. You will die."

He fired. Wyatt's coattails evaporated into swirling shreds as he took deliberate aim with his own shotgun. Hissing through his teeth, he said, "No."

And with that Wyatt fired both barrels. Curly Bill's midsection disappeared, the huge double charge of buckshot ripping him in half. The other cowboys flinched as they were sprayed with flecks of blood and gore.

One of the cowboys screamed, "Oh, my God, I've got his brains on me."

Wyatt was still moving forward, saying, "No."

His eyes burning like twin hells, Wyatt pulled his Buntline Special and fired. A cowboy fell over. Wyatt fired again. Another cowboy dropped. The others recoiled. Their faces looked like they were living in a walking nightmare as Wyatt, still firing, advanced on them.

Another cowboy went down.

Now Doc Holliday leaped up from the rocks, gun in hand, and yelled at the other three, "Come on."

They all rose as one and began to open fire, advancing four abreast. A wall of open gunfire drove the other cowboys off. They went running for their horses. Wyatt kept snapping his empty gun as the others came up to him.

He was like a man in a dream. He kept repeating over and over, "No . . . No . . . No . . ."

Doc took him gently by the hand and led him to a nearby rock, sitting Wyatt down and examining him. He ran his hand all over his body. The others were still firing at the cowboys as they retreated on horseback.

Doc said, "My God, Wyatt. You are shot to pieces."

Wyatt just said, "No."

Vermillion said to the cowboys, still within earshot, "Yeah, you better run, you bastards." Johnson came up to Doc Holliday and said, "How is he?"

Doc just said, "I don't believe it. He's clean."

Johnson's face was disbelieving. "What? I don't believe it. I saw the gun."

They examined him from the bottom of his shot-off boot heel to the top of his head. There was not a sign of a bullet hole, not even a scratch. As they searched, Wyatt began to tremble.

In a low voice, he said, "Morgan . . . Morgan . . . Virgil . . ."

The others stood looking at him, commiserating with him, understanding his loss. But none of them could understand how he could have walked through the hail of bullets and come out without a scratch.

They watched as Wyatt sat there, his face blank, his mind still far away.

Doc said, "If I hadn't've seen it with my own eyes, I wouldn't have believed it."

Turkey Jack Johnson said, "Do ya suppose he knows what he's done?"

Doc said, "I've seen men get like that and nothing could stop them. I believe they could have hit him and nothing could have stopped him. I believe that Curly Bill could have let go of both barrels of his shotgun into Wyatt and he would have still kept on going. Sometimes the spirit is stronger than the flesh."

Doc stopped and laughed. He said, "Well, that's a statement that I never thought I'd hear myself make."

McMasters said, "Well, Doc, maybe you are not as much of a cynic as you think you are."

Turkey Jack Johnson said, "Well, I for one am never going to tell anyone about this. They would never sell me another drink."

Vermillion laughed. "That's not a bad idea. Right now, why don't we all try to get a drink in us and maybe try to get Wyatt to come back to the land of the living. Lord, he is as pale as a ghost."

Doc said, "Don't be too sure he's not one right now."

Chapter Ten

It was almost twenty-four hours later and Wyatt had returned to himself. He and his four deputies had made a cold camp atop a little knoll about fifteen miles east of Tombstone.

Wyatt sat a short way away from the others. His thoughts lay on his brother Virgil, on his brother Morgan, on Mattie, and Virgil's and Morgan's wives, but most of all, on Josephine Marcus.

He remembered that awful moment when he had to protect her, and to prevent her from being recognized as something valuable to him by Curly Bill and the rest of the cowboys. Protect her from becoming a pawn in the terrible game against him.

That awful moment when he had called her a whore and a slut had forced her away from him.

He gazed off into the evening sky. Night was coming fast. Here and there he could see the twinkle of either campfires or lights. In the clear desert air, it was difficult to know how far away the lights were. They could have been a mile, they could have been thirty miles.

They themselves had made no campfire. They had made a supper of beef jerky and cold canned beans and cold biscuits. It had been almost three weeks since they last set out on the trail of the cowboys. On the deadly earnest business of removing them from the face of the earth.

Wyatt had calculated that they had cut the outlaws' number better than in half. He couldn't be sure, but he supposed that the weaker souls might have chosen desertion as the better part of valor.

But he knew good and well that Johnny Ringo had not deserted and Johnny Ringo was the man that he was most after now that Curly Bill and Floren Florentino were dead. He loomed like a specter in front of Wyatt's inner eye, a hazy specter, like a spirit in the sky. Wyatt couldn't quite draw a bead on him with his revolver.

The other men lay around the fireless camp in various states of exhaustion. It had been a long and hard trail. There had been very few nights when any of them had laid their heads on a pillow or their body on a bed, other than the hard-packed dirt of the desert. Surprisingly, Doc Holliday seemed to bear up better than the rest of them in the hardships. But then again, you never could tell with Doc. He might have been on the point of death and all you would get out of him would be a cynical answer or some cheerful nonsensical remark.

Johnson said, "I don't see how much longer we can keep racing around this country. Our horses are getting worn down, we're getting worn down. I've changed mounts twice, I guess the rest of them have about the same amount of times. Doesn't that black horse of yours ever give out?"

Wyatt said, "It's the Morgan blood in him. He's bred for

endurance. He gets that quick speed from the quarter horse in him, but that Kentucky Morgan blood gives him that endurance. If he don't work a full day, he thinks that he has been cheated. And he likes night work especially."

Turkey Jack Johnson laughed. He said, "Hell, he ought to. He's invisible in the dark."

Doc was smoking a small cigar. He said, "Turkey, that is a mistake that many a dead man has made. No one is invisible in the dark. Except the spirits."

Turkey Jack said, "Now, Doc, don't start talking about those damned spirits again. Every time you do, you scare me to death. Well, sometimes I look at you and I think I'm looking at one, as gaunt and wore out as you're looking these days."

Doc cackled. He said, "Ahhh, that's the illusion. Illusions can be tricky, you know. Have you ever considered that you might not even be here right now?"

"See, that's just what I mean. You are always talking like that and you are always scaring the hell out of me. I swear to heaven, I'd rather go up against ten of those cowboys with drawn guns and shotguns than listen to you talk in the dark for two minutes."

Wyatt laughed. He said, "We'd better get some sleep. We've got to try to cut their trails somewhere. They seem to have moved and left no forwarding address. They're not using that roost anymore on top of the purple hills. Frank, where do you suppose Ringo would lead them?"

Frank McMasters looked thoughtful for a moment. He said, "Wyatt, that is a question that only Johnny Ringo could answer. This is a man that is hard to figure, I've got to tell ya. The one thing that you can expect him to do is to do the unexpected."

Wyatt said, "Do you think he is still in the area?"

McMasters said, "I *know* that he is somewhere in the area. In fact, he could be a hundred yards from us right now, the whole bunch of them creeping up on us. He's not a man that is going to leave the field of battle unless he is either dead or has won."

Doc Holliday said, "I admire valor, especially in my dead enemies."

Wyatt said, "All right, let's cut the foolishness. I reckon we had all better get some shut-eye. I'd like to be up at four and get out early. Maybe they will make a breakfast fire and we will be able to see the smoke against the morning sun."

Without saying another word, the five lawmen rolled themselves in their blankets.

Doc said, "I never can sleep anyway, so I'll take the first watch. Turkey, I'll call you in two hours."

There were a few mumbled good nights and then everyone but Doc drifted off to sleep. For a long time he lay there, quietly smoking his cigar and staring up at the night sky, where the stars glittered like bright pebbles against the black velvet background.

He said, "Ah, eternity, eternity. Why must you be so long? You have no end. You just stretch on and on. Will I be a part of you, eternity?"

It was morning and Johnny Ringo was crouched by the fire with the other cowboys. His face was a deeply shadowed mask. The two Iron Springs survivors stood before him. One of them was Bob Ward, who seemed to lead a charmed life. He had escaped this time, not because of generosity on Wyatt's part, but because he had been hanging back and was able to slip away in darkness when the heavy fire began.

The other was a grizzled veteran of the cowboy band. A

bearded man named Schmidt. He, too, had chosen desertion as the better part of valor. He and Bob Ward had found each other in the night and had made straight for the main cowboy camp, which had been moved ten miles nearer the Mexican border amid the clutter of buttes and slashes and crevices and other rough country.

They had told their story and now Ward told it again. "We hit him half a dozen times, but he just kept coming. Walked right up to Curly Bill with that big shotgun and blew him up."

Ringo said, "Are you sure it was Curly Bill? Are you sure he killed Curly Bill?" As he said it Ringo started making strange inarticulate sounds, inhaling and exhaling like an animal. His eyes almost swam in panic. He growled deep in his throat.

He said, "I can't believe he killed Curly Bill. He couldn't have."

Ward said, "Ringo, he didn't just kill him. He burned him down . . . but it was his face. You should have seen the man's face. You should have seen Wyatt's face. You should have seen the way he kept coming. I swear we hit him. I swear we hit him over and over again, but he just kept coming."

Ringo said, "I don't want to hear that stuff. He's just a man."

"But you didn't see his face."

Ringo looked up, suddenly deadly calm, his face a blank. He said, "You see my face, don't you?"

They nodded. Ward said, "Of course we see your face. What're you talking about?"

Ringo said, "This."

Without saying another word, he drew his gun and fired two shots so quickly, they sounded like one. A bullet found a home in the forehead of each of the survivors. Bob Ward and Schmidt dropped at almost the same time. The other cowboys jumped, startled by the insane brutality of what they had just witnessed. Ringo stood up. He was in full possession of the situation. He was now the new leader, he was fearsome, he was matchless, he was insane.

Ringo said, "Now everybody get this through their heads. Wyatt Earp dies and the rest of the deputies die with him. I'm running this show now and I'm telling you, Earp dies, they all die, understand? We're gonna kill them for what they did to Curly Bill. We're gonna ride them into the ground and slaughter 'em like rabbits. 'Cause this is my time, children. This is where I get woolly. And any one of you that flinches or backs away will have me to answer to. Do you understand that?"

His eyes slowly rolled across the faces of the men before him. Some blinked and looked away, some ducked their heads. All of them understood his message.

About midmorning, Wyatt and his men came across a small spring-fed creek and decided to take a break. They needed it, and their horses needed it even more.

The day was warm, not a cloud in the sky. Soon it would be June, and hotter still.

Wyatt was down at the creek monitoring the horses as they watered. He was careful that they should not get too much. Up above, on a little rise, Doc Holliday, Johnson, Vermillion, and McMasters sat around a small smokeless campfire. They had brewed a much-needed pot of coffee, and as they waited for it to boil they talked in hushed, almost reverent tones.

They were still talking about Wyatt walking through the hail of bullets to kill Curly Bill and to rout the cowboys. It was a scene that none of them could shake from their minds, no matter how hard they tried.

Vermillion said, "You ever seen anything like that before? I reckon I could live to be four hundred years old and I'd never expected to see anything like it."

Johnson said, "I've never heard of anything like it, nor anybody that had heard of anything like it, nor anybody who knew anybody who knew anybody who had ever heard of anything like it."

Frank McMasters said, looking around, "Where's Wyatt?"

Doc said lightly, "Oh, he's down at the creek, walking on water."

McMasters said, "Well, he better have another miracle up his sleeve, 'cuz I know Ringo. He'll be coming."

"Where is the smart money on this, Doc? How far away do you think Ringo is?" McMasters asked.

Doc said, "Anything I say, of course, will be pure conjecture. But I would say that within sight of five hours, either we will sight him or he will sight us. But of course, McMasters would be more of an authority on that subject than I. What say you, Frank?"

McMasters said, "Sounds just about right." He nodded. "There's just so much of his desert for us to run around in. They're not gonna cross over into Mexico. They're not gonna go back to Tombstone. They've got to stay within range of the water holes. I think we're playing ring-around-a-rosy out here around these buttes and mountains, and first one thing then another. What do you think Wyatt's figuring on? You reckon he plans to go straight at them?"

Doc said, "I would be sure that that would be his preference, especially given his history. Especially the history of the night before last. I don't believe that I've ever seen a finer example of a man going straight at someone than that."

Johnson said, "Well, I don't know how much more of this these horses can take. I know that mine don't have a couple more hours in him. But I'll tell you this. Whatever Wyatt wants to do, I'll do it."

Vermillion nodded. He said, "Amen on that."

McMasters said, "If it was my brother, I'd want revenge too."

Doc Holliday shook his head and felt in his coat pocket until he came upon his silver flask. He unscrewed the cap and took a quick drink. He was beginning to tremble when he said, "Gentlemen, don't misunderstand. It isn't vengeance that he's after. It's a reckoning. He wants to reckon up the score."

The words were barely out of his mouth before he started into a heavy fit of coughing. He hacked into his handkerchief and tucked it into his pocket. There was a low rumble in his chest as he fought away another cough. He jerked the flask out of his pocket and took another quick drink.

McMasters said, "Doc, you oughta be in bed. Why in the hell are you doing this?"

Doc was still gasping for breath. It took him a moment to answer. He said, "Because Wyatt Earp is my friend."

Johnson said, "Hell, I've got lots of friends."

Doc turned on him, glaring. He said, "I don't."

Wyatt came walking back up. He had left the horses down at the creek. The coffee had boiled and the others had poured themselves a cup.

Turkey Jack, using his hat for a pot holder, took hold of the big tin pot and poured Wyatt a big steamy cup. He handed it up to him from his seat on the ground.

Wyatt said, "Thanks." For a moment he stood looking

around at the surrounding countryside. He said, "What do yall think?"

They shrugged. McMasters said, "Wyatt, the horses are playing out. I think we're willing, but I don't know how much longer the horses can go."

Wyatt nodded slowly. "What's making it so hard is that they won't establish a base camp. I guess we'll have to go around this afternoon, and if we don't come up with anything, I think we'll have to go back into Tombstone and get more horses. Even my black is starting to labor."

The men nodded. It was clear that something had to be done. They were almost out of food, out of patience, and nearly out of horses.

For four long, hot, sweaty hours, they had searched fruitlessly for any sign of Johnny Ringo and the other remaining cowboys.

Late in the afternoon they found themselves atop a plateau with a good view in all directions. As they gazed around, heat waves shimmered up from the desert floor, making them see things that weren't there, making mountains suddenly appear, making buttes appear much closer, making shimmering lakes in the sea of sand.

Turkey Johnson said, "Look yonder. What's that—" He stopped. "Aw hell, it's nothing. Looked like a big white house out there for a moment." He laughed. "I don't reckon you'll see any big white houses out here, not with that sand blasting the paint off as fast as it would."

McMasters said, "I thought I saw something moving just beyond that far butte over there. There to the south. Take a look."

They all strained their eyes, staring in the direction that he had indicated.

Vermillion said, "Aw, Frank, you just seeing a giant jackrabbit moving around."

But then Wyatt said, "No, no. It is men. It's a band of horsemen. Look, they're coming our way."

They sat on their horses, motionless, and watched as the outlaws came straight toward their position. They were aware that they were outlined against the sky atop the plateau, but it was too late now to hide themselves. Besides, Wyatt had no intention of hiding. They watched as the outlaws came closer and closer. Now they appeared only a mile or two off. He looked at the flat desert around them.

He said, "Boys, if they keep coming like they are, we can ford up on top of this rise and play merry hell with them. We might not hit them from this distance, but we can damn sure leave a lot of them afoot on the desert. What do yall think?"

Frank McMasters was frowning. He said, "Something looks funny. I'm pretty sure that's Ringo out in front, but I'll be damned if I don't think that's John Behan with him."

Turkey Johnson said, "Aw hell, the sheriff? What would he be doing with them?"

Vermillion said, "I wouldn't put it past the bastard, but by what act of law does he join up with those damn coyotes and sidewinders and scum and curs?"

McMasters said, "I've got to look at this a little closer." He turned and reached back in his saddlebags, coming out with his binoculars. He put the glasses to his eyes and sighted the men while his horse shifted nervously beneath him.

After a moment he said, "Well, I'll be damned. I'll just go all to hell."

Wyatt asked, "What?"

"You ain't gonna believe it, but they are wearing badges.

Deputy-sheriff badges. Every last damned man jack of 'em."

Turkey Jack Johnson said, "Son of a bitch."

Wyatt said, "Are you sure? Can there be no mistake?"

McMasters peered closely through his binoculars and then shook his head. He said, "There's no mistake. Hell, Billy Breakenridge is with him too." He laughed.

Johnson said, "Hell, that sissy boy? He's with him too? He's out in the desert this far?"

Jack Vermillion said, "Well, now I've heard everything. Billy Breakenridge?"

McMasters said, "Ain't nobody but."

Wyatt said, "We had better dismount. I think we got trouble coming. We better get ready for it."

Frank McMasters said, "Wyatt, are you sure it's a good idea to fort up here? I mean, there's a bunch of them and there is only five of us. And there ain't much cover up here as it looks. They make a charge at us up that slope to the south, and they will be in amongst us before we know what's happening."

Wyatt said, "I don't see how we could very well run."

McMasters said, "They might not have seen us. The sun's behind us. Why don't we just try to ease down the left side of this plateau and see what happens."

Wyatt looked around at the other men. One by one they nodded. He rubbed his jaw. "I don't know," he said.

Doc coughed and put his handkerchief to his mouth. When the spasm had passed, he said, "Wyatt, my boy, it won't be of much value to you revenge-wise if we are all dead and they are still alive. The old adage is that it is better to live to be able to fight another day. I don't think that this is the ground that you want to fight them on."

Wyatt nodded. He had never heard Doc Holliday give bad

advice, especially when it came to a fight or a poker game. He said, "How're the horses?"

Turkey Johnson shook his head and said, "Mine's finished. He sure as hell ain't in no shape for no running fight."

McMasters said, "Mine's about the same."

Wyatt said, "Let's mount up and get off this thing by the west slope. We'll try to head for that clutter of little hills back there and try to fort up there. First let's make sure if they've seen us or not."

Without another word, they mounted up and started down the gentle little slope toward the west. They had barely reached the level plain of the desert when Doc suddenly looked very sick.

He began to cough and to sway dizzily in the saddle.

Wyatt came up beside him and dismounted and reached up for him. Doc said, "Just don't touch me. Don't touch me. Dammit. Come on, let's go. I . . ." He turned his horse as if to ride away and fainted dead away.

Wyatt said, "Grab him."

They all reached up and grabbed the frail body as Doc Holliday fell out of his saddle. They eased him to the ground.

It had been a hard two hours' ride in the late afternoon and early evening as they made their way across the Arizona desert, supporting a very sick Doc Holliday in the saddle. Just as the light began to fail they spotted a ranch house up ahead. Jack Vermillion recognized it as belonging to a rancher named Joe Hooker.

He said, "I know Joe Hooker. He's a good man. Any enemy of the cowboys is a friend of his."

Wyatt said, "Then how has he held on this long against them without cutting some kind of deal?"

Vermillion said, "I think it's because he don't have enough for them to want or enough for them to pay the price that he will extract. He's got three good sons and every one of them can fire a gun, and Joe Hooker ain't no slouch himself. He's just barely making a living, but it's his living and he damned well intends to keep it."

Wyatt said, "Do you think he will take us in?"

Vermillion said, "Of course, Wyatt, he'll take us in. He's a good man and he'd damn sure take us in."

Wyatt looked over at his sick friend. Doc Holliday was barely able to stay in the saddle, even with help. There was blood all down the front of his white shirt, and every few moments he was racked with a terrible coughing fit. They had tried to get as much whiskey down him as they could, which seemed to relax his spasms of coughing.

Wyatt said, "We'd better head down that way. I sure as hell hope that Johnny Ringo and his friend John Behan didn't spot us. What do you think, Frank?"

Frank McMasters said, "I don't know, Wyatt. There is no way to know. The only way we'll know is if he attacks us."

As they rode toward the ranch house Wyatt said, "Well, Mr. Hooker's ranch ain't exactly my idea of the best place to fort up, but I don't guess we've got any choice. Doc has got to have some rest. He's got to have some help."

As they approached the ranch, Joe Hooker and his three grown sons rode out to meet them. They came toward Wyatt and his party cautiously. "That's Wyatt Earp. Yeah, that's Wyatt Earp. He's a U. S. marshal."

They came forward quickly, pulling up as they neared.

Joe Hooker said, "Howdy, Marshal Earp."

Wyatt just nodded. He said, "We've got a mighty sick man with us."

Hooker said, "You can put him up in my ranch if you want."

Wyatt said, "I think I ought to warn you, Mr. Hooker, that some of the red sashes, the cowboys, with Johnny Ringo at their head, could be on our trail. There could be trouble. We could ride on. We don't want to bring you down any trouble."

Joe Hooker just shook his head and said, "They're trouble anywhere, anytime, anyplace. If there's to be trouble with these boys, I'd much rather have you and your boys with us. No, you all come ahead. I can see how sick that man is. That's . . . that's Doc Holliday, ain't it?"

Wyatt nodded slowly. "Yes, it is."

One of Hooker's sons said, almost in awe, "I was in town the day that yall had the fight at the O.K. Corral. I never saw anything like it in my life."

Wyatt looked down at the ground. He didn't speak.

Mr. Hooker said, "Son, Mr. Earp doesn't want to talk about that stuff right now. He's got a sick friend. Let's get him on up to the house."

Together they joined in the group and rode at a slow pace to favor the ailing Doc Holliday. They dismounted in front of the ranch house. Wyatt and Frank McMasters half carried and half helped Doc into the house. Joe Hooker led the way. His wife came running from the kitchen, flour on the front of her apron.

She said, "Oh my. Oh my. That poor man. Is he shot?"

Wyatt just shook his head. He said, "No, ma'am. He's coughing up blood. It's his lungs."

She said, "Oh, let me get a bed ready."

Wyatt said, "Ma'am, we need to get him laying down pretty quick."

She said, "Just lay him down in here." She led the way into a spare bedroom where three cots were set up.

With gentleness and care, Wyatt and Frank McMasters eased Doc down on the bed. The others crowded into the doorway to watch.

Hooker said, "I'm no doctor, except where horses and cattle are concerned, but he looks mighty bad."

His face creased with worry, Wyatt sat down next to Doc on the bed. He said to Mrs. Hooker, "Ma'am, I need some pillows to prop his head up with, please. It helps ease his coughing."

She ran and collected pillows off of the other beds and then helped Wyatt prop Doc up on the bed. His head rocked back and forth, his eyes were slits.

Doc said, the words barely audible, "Not sick . . . not sick. Let me get up."

Wyatt looked up at Hooker. He said, "Do you have such things as whiskey in the house?"

Joe Hooker said, "I've got a brand-new bottle of bourbon. I'll get it."

He hurried out of the room and was back in a moment with both the bottle and a glass. Wyatt filled half the water glass and held Doc's head in one hand while he put the rim of the glass to Doc's lips with the other. Doc sucked the whiskey down greedily. He took the full measure and then lay back.

He said hoarsely, "Thanks. Makes it hurt less."

Frank McMasters shook his head. He said, "I can't say for sure, Turkey, but if I were getting a bet down on it, it would be that they saw us with Doc sick as he was. We wasn't making no tracks and we were sure as hell leaving a trail behind us. Ringo is as mean as a rattlesnake and he sure as hell ain't stupid."

Turkey Johnson looked around. He said, "Then you figure we better get ready to fight?"

McMasters nodded. "I reckon we had better get the horses put up and find out how much ammo that Mr. Hooker and the boys have. We're liable to find out how good of shots they are right quick."

Frank McMasters had been correct. Johnny Ringo and the rest of the cowboys had cut the trail of Wyatt and the rest of his deputies. They had followed in behind and were steadily gaining on the five lawmen when a serious mischance delayed them and caused them to lose the trail and even caused them to lose their interest in the immediate pursuit of Wyatt Earp and the others.

They had come around a little butte and had seen in the distance the body of a stagecoach.

It was John Behan who had pointed and had said, "What the hell is that? That looks like the westbound stage. But where the hell are the horses?"

Johnny Ringo said, "Who the hell cares? I'm after Wyatt Earp."

John Behan for once asserted some authority. He said, "I am still the sheriff of this county, and I have to go and investigate that stagecoach." He turned his horse in that direction and Johnny Ringo and the rest of the cowboys reluctantly followed. They rode at a trot, the distance narrowing rapidly.

As they got closer they could see that the traces had been cut and that the horses were gone. They could see that the driver and the shotgun rider were lying on the ground. Then they were close enough to see the bullet holes in the body of the stagecoach.

John Behan rode straight up to where one of the doors of

the stagecoach was open. He gasped when he saw that it was the acting troupe. They had closed their engagement in Tombstone and were leaving for another booking.

Inside, John saw Josephine Marcus sitting in the corner, her face white, her hands trembling. She stared as in her arms she cradled the lifeless body of the thespian Fabian.

He lay full length on the seat, looking like the dying Hamlet, except that he was already dead. His white shirt was soaked in his blood from the bullet hole that had pierced him through and through.

At the door, John Behan left his horse and thrust his head inside. He said, "Oh no. My God, Josephine. Are you all right?"

Josephine Marcus said, her voice dead, "What do you care? It was your friends that did this to us."

For a second John Behan couldn't respond. He pulled his hat back and turned away from them. His deputy, Billy Breakenridge, looked into the coach and was crushed at the sight of Fabian's lifeless form. Tears formed in his eyes.

He said, "Oh no. That beautiful man. What a terrible waste." In a lifeless voice, almost as if she was reciting the words from a play, Josephine said, "We were headed for another booking. They tried to take my watch. Then . . ." She paused and looked at Fabian. "He cursed them for being cowards and then they shot him. This beautiful, lovely man—they shot him. They shot him dead. They just did it and then they rode off."

Tears slowly coursed down her cheeks. She said, "He may have been vain and an actor, but he was better than all of you. And gentler and braver. I don't understand any of this. I only know that it is ugly. It's a sin, it's vile, it's vicious."

She let her eyes move to the outside of the coach, looking

from face to face of the many cowboys. Her voice grew stronger. She said, "You're all ugly and he was beautiful. He came into your ugly world and you killed him for it. Anyway, the ones that did it headed north, not that you care."

Breakenridge reached out and carefully touched Fabian's forehead. He recoiled, for it was cold.

Josephine said, "Yes, he's dead. He's been dead for several hours. He's already growing stiff. Are you happy?"

Breakenridge staggered backward and put his hands to his face. He just stood there.

Inside the coach, the other actors were still. No one moved. They were in shock.

John Behan turned to Ringo. He said, "Dammit, Ringo, I never counted on this. This is too much. I said I would help you with the Earps, but this is too much. This is not going to work. I can't have this. Dammit, I'm the sheriff of this county. You can't kill people like this."

Ringo shrugged. He said, "I didn't have anything to do with it."

"It was cowboys that killed him, obviously. Who else could it have been?"

From the coach, Josephine said in a loud voice, "There were two of them and they both wore red sashes. They were of you, they were part of you, they were ugly as you, they were as obscene as you."

Johnny Ringo said to Sheriff Behan, "Most likely it was Claibourne and Fuller. They cut out and split a few days back. Said they had had enough. Said that they were going to Mexico. I reckon it was them trying to make one last payday. They picked a hell of a time to do it. Wonder if there was any money on that coach."

Behan said, "How can you talk about that at a time like this? This can't be. We've got to go after them."

Ringo said, "I'm after the Earps."

Behan said, "Not now you're not. Not until we get this mess cleared up."

Before Ringo could answer, they were startled to see Billy Breakenridge mount up and start his horse toward the north.

Ringo said, "Where the hell do you think you're going? Get back here."

The little deputy straightened up his spectacles and turned to his boss, Sheriff Behan. He said, "I'm not going with you."

Behan sputtered, "What the hell you talking about? Of course you are going with us. You are my deputy."

Billy said, "I'm sorry, sir. But we have got to have some law." He started to ride off.

Sheriff Behan yelled after him, "Billy, get back here."

Billy continued to ride north, not looking back.

Ringo laughed and said, "Let the sissy boy go. We don't need him."

One of the actors, the juggler, who looked much plainer off stage, came struggling out of the coach. He said, "The least you can do is round up the stagecoach horses and not leave us stranded out here. We're miles from nowhere. We ask for nothing more."

Johnny Ringo said, "Oh, the hell with you. Walk."

Sheriff Behan said, "You will have horses."

He turned to Ringo and said, "Dismount four of your men and hook those horses into those traces and put a man up there to drive."

The juggler said, "I can drive the horses. I don't think we want any more help from you. If you will just be good enough to get us the horses back, we'll be good enough to be on our way. All we have to do is follow the road."

Behan turned again to Johnny Ringo. He said, "Dismount your men, Mr. Ringo."

Ringo stared back at him for a moment. He said grimly, "I don't know who you're talking to, Behan, but you're walking on mighty thin ice."

For once, Behan was showing some backbone. "If you don't, I will take back every badge you and your men are wearing. Now then, sir, you will then be going after federal marshals as outlaws, and if you harm them without the authority I have invested you with, you will have broken federal laws and you will have United States federal marshals descend on you like snow on a mountaintop. Do I make myself clear, sir?"

Johnny Ringo stared back, his mind working. He realized that what Behan said was true, but he could not let it pass without a sneering remark. He said, "You're doing it for her, aren't you?" He nodded his head at the coach where Josephine sat.

Behan said, "Whatever the reason, you will do it."

Ringo said, "You know she don't care for you. You know that it's Earp for her, don't you?"

Behan just stared back at Ringo. He said, "Are you going to dismount your men or are you going to round up the stagecoach horses, or what? I'll give you thirty seconds to make up your mind or I'll take those badges back."

"We could just kill you," Ringo said softly.

"No, Ringo, you won't do that. I know too much about you. There are too many papers in my office about you. You're not going to kill me, Ringo. If you were, you would have done it a long time ago."

Ringo made a circling motion with his arm in the air and

said, "Scout around and bring in those coach horses. And hurry up about it, we're wasting time."

It was still a matter of more than two hours before the cowboys were able to locate the stagecoach horses, drive them in, and then get them hooked into the harnesses, some of which they had to repair. When it was finally done, it was good and dark. The juggler climbed up into the driver's seat.

Sheriff Behan said, "Are you sure that you can handle this team?"

The juggler looked down at him and said, "If I can handle juggling wooden Indian clubs, I reckon I can juggle these horses. I wasn't always on the stage, Sheriff. And by the way, we are obliged to you for saving our lives."

Ringo and Behan watched as the coach slowly jolted off toward the west. The little road lay dim in the coming darkness. Behan's heart ached with wanting to go with them, to protect Josephine, but he knew that such a sign of weakness in front of the cowboys would be badly misinterpreted.

He turned to Ringo and said, "All right, now what?"

For a moment Ringo stood silent in the dark. He said, "Well, it's clear that we've lost Earp's tracks for the time being. No use fumbling around in the dark like a bunch of damned fools."

John Behan in a choking voice said, "I never got the chance to tell her that it wasn't us. That it was Bill Claibourne and Wes Fuller. Now she will always think that I had a hand in it."

Ringo laughed loud and hard. He said, "Behan, you're a joke, just a damn joke."

It was late at night, but through the darkness the driver spotted the solitary light in the distance. It was the light in the bedroom of the Hooker house, where Wyatt and his deputies were sitting up with Doc Holliday. To the juggler, it was a beacon of hope.

He called down to the others, "I think I see help ahead. We may get there by dawn." He slapped the horses and they charged forward through the dusty, loose sand of the desert road. They were a long hour getting there.

It was still dark as they arrived. The juggler hollered out, "Hello in the house. Hello in the house."

He was unaware that all around him, men were hidden with guns aimed directly at him. For all they knew, the coach could be a Trojan horse full of cowboys.

From the porch, Wyatt recognized the juggler and walked out eagerly. Joe Hooker followed him out onto the porch. The juggler jumped down from the driver's seat.

"We had a holdup. Our horses are nearly out of water."

Wyatt said, "What . . . what happened?" His thoughts went immediately to Josephine.

The driver said, "They killed the driver and the shotgun man and they killed Fabian."

Wyatt was almost afraid to ask the next question. Before he could form the words, Josephine emerged from the coach. Wyatt stared at her for a long moment. She, too, froze, holding his gaze. He walked up to her, his hand unconsciously reaching out to touch her shoulder.

He said, "Hello."

It was but one word, but there was a world of meaning in it. She said, "Oh, Wyatt." She fell into his arms.

For a long moment they clung to each other before she pulled back with tears in her eyes. She said, "They killed Fabian. Those animals. They killed that poor, gentle, kind man."

Wyatt looked inside the coach. Fabian lay on one seat; the other actors huddled close on the other bench.

He turned back to Josephine. He said, "It doesn't surprise me, dear. I'm very sorry about your friend." He paused. "And I'm very sorry about . . ."

Before he could go on, Josephine said, "I forgave you the minute that you said it."

Wyatt was startled. He said, "You did? How could you have known?"

She smiled and said, "I know you and I know why you did it. I thank you for it."

"You thank me? Oh, my God. How much I thank you."

Just then Joe Hooker came by. He said, "I've been talking to the driver. I told him that I did not think it was safe for them to stay here. What do you think?"

Wyatt jerked his head up. He said, "Yeah, you're right. Ringo and the rest will be here soon enough. This place will be about as safe as the middle of a pitched dagger."

He turned to Josephine. He said, "You've gotta go on."

She said, "But what about us?"

"I'll find you."

"How?" she asked.

"Don't worry. I'm not ever going to lose you again."

The juggler had climbed back up on the driver's seat. He said, "Marshal Earp, if we're going, we're gonna have to get on the move."

Wyatt turned back to Josephine and said, "Josephine, get back into the coach." He took her by the arm and helped her into the coach and then shut the door.

She leaned out the window, stretching her hands toward him. He touched her hand to his lips and said, "Good-bye, for now."

Then he stepped back and yelled at the driver, "Get those

horses out of here. You've got to make some miles. It will be light soon and you'll be all right."

For a long moment Wyatt stood in the yard of the ranch and watched the stagecoach go off into the distance, watched as it got smaller and smaller.

Then he turned back to the ranch house, where Hooker, Turkey, Vermillion, and McMasters stood and said, "Well, I wonder how Doc's doing?"

Morning came and went and Doc didn't seem to improve. Toward noonday, Mrs. Hooker was able to get a little broth down him. In the middle of the afternoon, Doc was asking for a little whiskey. By early in the evening, he started making jokes.

Wyatt got up and said, "Hell, he's all right."

McMasters said, "Son of a bitch is too mean to die."

That night, Wyatt sat on the bed in Doc's room while Doc stood in front of the mirror with a bowl of water and shaved. Wyatt was recounting the sudden appearance of the stagecoach and Josephine that morning. He had already told Doc that his heart had leaped at the sight of her.

He said, "But, God, you should have seen how she breezed out of here, like she had wings. Funny thing, but I can't remember really how she looked. I can remember parts of her as clear as crystal. Her mouth, her walk, how she shut her eyes when she laughed. Little bits and pieces, but not the whole package. I can't put it together, for some reason. But, oh God, the sight of her. Doc, it made me tremble all over, and Doc, you know that I'm not a sentimental man."

Doc turned away from shaving and looked back at Wyatt. He said in his most cynical voice, "Oh, God. You're really in—"

Wyatt cut him off. He said, "In spades, Doc. In spades.

I'm in love with every second of her life. Every inch of her. Hell, I'll probably love her when I'm dust."

Doc said, "Good God. And another man bites the dust. Literally."

It was a cold morning in the hollow of a few small hills. Wrapped in blankets, Wes Fuller and Billy Claibourne sipped coffee before a dying fire.

Fuller said, "We'd better put out this damn fire pretty soon. It's getting light and I don't want them to see the smoke. It would show up against this clear sky."

Claibourne said, "I'm doing it . . . I'm doing it."

With a branch he spread the smoldering coals, heaping sand over them with his free hand. Behind them there was a sudden sound. Both of them jumped up.

"Who's that?" Fuller asked.

Billy Breakenridge quickly stepped into the camp. He had his Winchester at his shoulder, squinting through his spectacles. He said, "It's Deputy Breakenridge."

Fuller and Claibourne relaxed and lowered the pistols they had drawn. They laughed and heaved sighs of relief.

"Sister boy. Thank God, we was afraid—" said Fuller.

"You shouldn't have killed Mr. Fabian. You shouldn't have done that. It was wrong. I'm taking you both in for that."

Fuller said, "What? You've gotta be kidding me? Look, just go on home before you get hurt."

Billy Breakenridge said, "Don't want to kill ya, but I will if'n I have to. I'm warning you for the last time."

Claibourne said, "No, I'm warning you, sister boy." He stepped forward menacingly.

Breakenridge tensed. He said, "Don't try it. Just don't try it, Claibourne."

Claibourne drew his pistol deliberately. The sight made Breakenridge recoil in fright. He stumbled backward and his rifle accidently fired. With a surprised look on his face, Claibourne put a hand to his chest. Blood leaked through his fingers. He staggered sideways and then fell, a look of utter disbelief in his eyes.

Fuller looked at him in shock and then turned on Breakenridge and raised his gun. Breakenridge fired again; this time it was not an accident. Fuller grabbed his midsection, dropping his gun and stumbling backward. He fell to his knees. He looked up at Breakenridge.

Breakenridge shrugged. He said timidly, "Sorry."

For a moment Fuller worked his mouth, but no sound came out. Finally, like a tree falling in the forest, he keeled over on his side. After a moment he stopped breathing. Breakenridge stared down at the bodies and shrugged.

He said, "Guess they won't be calling me sister no longer."

Then, as if nothing had happened, he began resurrecting their fire and righting the coffeepot on the fire. He found one of their cups and looked into it. He took the tail of his shirt, scrubbed it out, and then poured himself a cup of coffee. He sat there calmly, sipping the coffee and looking at the dead bodies. He was already thinking about what a chore it was going to be to lift the bodies up on the horses and sling them sideways so that he could bring them back into town.

It was his first arrest.

Chapter Eleven

Wyatt and Joe Hooker sat out in the front yard of the ranch. They were warned by a ranch hand that a rider was approaching, leading two horses that were loaded with what the cowhand termed "vulture meat."

It was a hot day. Both men were sweaty. They had just gotten up from the lunch table. As they watched, Frank McMasters came out of the ranch house and joined them.

They stood there, watching, as the rider approached. Finally, McMasters said, "That's Billy Breakenridge. He's got two dead bodies on those horses."

Wyatt said, "Reckon who they could be?"

McMasters said, "Don't know. Hard to tell from here."

Wyatt laughed softly. "Don't reckon it could be Johnny Ringo and John Behan, could it?"

McMasters said, "No such luck."

Joe Hooker said, "I thought your friend Doc Holliday was going to come around. He seems to have had a sinking spell."

Wyatt nodded. "He does that. Doc's dying. Should have

already been dead. A lesser man would have already given up, but he rallies from time to time."

He shaded his eyes with his hands. He said, "Yeah, Frank, that's Billy Breakenridge and he's towing some vulture meat on those two horses he's dragging. Who the hell could it be, and what is Billy Breakenridge doing with dead men? I thought he was scared of them."

McMasters said, "Billy Breakenridge's scared of everything."

They stood silent as Billy Breakenridge turned into the ranch yard, towing his grisly cargo. He rode straight toward them.

As he came toward them McMasters said, "Wes Fuller and Billy Claibourne."

Wyatt glanced over at him. "How can you tell—they're lying facedown?"

McMasters said, "I've seen them from the back also. Mostly in a fight when they were running away."

As Billy Breakenridge rode up, Wyatt said, "What you got there, Billy?"

"Like Frank said, I've got Wes Fuller and Billy Claibourne. They're my prisoners."

Wyatt smiled slowly. He said, "Don't look like they're giving you much trouble."

Billy said, "They robbed the stage. They killed one of them actors. That real nice, that real pretty one. They also killed the driver and the shotgun messenger. I arrested them."

Wyatt said, "Yeah, you really arrested them. They look good and arrested to me. What are you gonna do with them?"

Billy answered, "I'm taking them to Tombstone."

Wyatt nodded. "All right. I guess that might be the thing

to do, although they might stiffen up on you a mite before you get them in there. Did you consider just burying them out here in the desert somewhere?"

Billy said, "Naw, these here are my first arrests. I wanna show them off. I want the townspeople who have always laughed at me to see them. You know, I don't know why I've never made an arrest before. I kinda like it."

Wyatt glanced at Hooker and McMasters. He said, "Well, all right, Billy, I can see your point. Would you care to step down and have a bite of lunch? Or maybe even a drink?"

Billy adjusted his spectacles on his nose and said, "No, I reckon I better get to moving on. By the way, I think you ought to know that Ringo has a pretty good idea of where you are."

Wyatt spoke a little sadly. "I figured as much."

Billy said, "We was following your trail when we came upon the stagecoach. God, it was awful."

Wyatt said, "We know about the stagecoach, Billy. They came through last night. They're all all right. I'm sorry you feel bad about that nice actor."

Billy lifted his hat. He said, "You've always been a nice man, Marshal Earp. I always thought a great deal of you. I never showed it because I was afraid that you might misunderstand."

Wyatt just smiled.

Billy said, "If I's you, I wouldn't hang around here. You know Sheriff Behan deputized all those thieves and murdering outlaws. God knows why he would do something like that. You know, he's not law, Marshal Earp. He's not law at all. I'm ashamed to have worked for him this long. My eyes are open now. The scales have fallen. But they are headed this way. That stagecoach delayed them, but they'll be here, Marshal Earp."

Wyatt nodded. "Thank you very much, Billy. You have a good trip into Tombstone."

They watched as Billy reined his horse around and started on the ride to Tombstone.

But before he could get out of the gate, Wyatt called, "Deputy. Deputy Breakenridge."

Billy Breakenridge stopped his horse and looked back.

Wyatt smiled and nodded at him and lifted his thumb in salute and said, "Good work, Deputy."

Billy Breakenridge smiled and shifted, sitting taller in the saddle. He put the spurs to his horse and started all three of the animals out the yard gate at a trot.

Wyatt just shook his head. He said, "Strange things have been going on around here and they get stranger by the minute."

McMasters said, "Yeah, but they ain't anything like strange about Johnny Ringo. Listen, Wyatt, I don't think that we ought to be here when he comes. We don't have enough hands. Mr. Hooker, you say that you have about four hands besides your three sons and yourself."

Hooker nodded and said, "Yeah, but I wouldn't count on but maybe one or two of them in a gunfight. I'd say, really, there's the four or five of us and the four or five of you, depending on how Doc is."

Wyatt said, "I don't think that we better depend on Doc Holliday. I am afraid that he may be dealing his last hand."

The cowboys were camped on a hilltop overlooking Joe Hooker's ranch in the valley. Standing on the highest point, John Behan and Johnny Ringo looked down over the small spread.

As they were watching they saw a messenger on horseback working his way up the hill. He was waving a letter in his hand.

Johnny Ringo said, "I wonder who that could be from? Reckon it could be surrender terms from Wyatt Earp?"

Behan said, "Earp isn't going to surrender. You misjudge the man."

Ringo said, "I figure it was *him* asking us to surrender. We outnumber him at least three to one."

Behan looked at the man riding toward them now. He said, "No, I know that man. He's from the telegraph office. He's come out of Tombstone. That's . . . that's Fred Hardy, I think."

Ringo turned his attention back to the ranch. He said, "I think Hooker's got about four or five hands outside of his sons. Then there is the five of them including Wyatt. We could take them right enough that it might be a mess. I think what we will do is to keep the place bottled up for now and figure how to flush them. You know, we're down to about twenty-five or twenty-eight men now. I haven't taken a count lately."

Behan said, "I think one or two slipped away in the night."

Ringo bit his lip and said, "A real bunch of brave boys, I thought. Now, I don't reckon we had better rush them. That damned Doc Holliday can knock five men out of the saddle before the second hand of a watch can go from one number to another."

The messenger had come up to Behan by then and handed him the telegram. The sheriff opened it and read it quickly.

As he did he said, "Oh hell. Oh no. Dammit, dammit, dammit."

Ringo said, "What's the matter, you just find out that you're somebody's papa?"

Behan said, "This ain't funny, Johnny. This is too much. Things have gotten completely out of hand. Word has gotten back to the governor, Governor Gosper. He's talking about asking the president to send in the army. My God, Ringo, do you have any idea what that means? It means martial law."

He paused and thought for a minute. He turned to Ringo and said, "Listen, Ringo, you can't hesitate. You've got to get this over with, one way or another. You can't sit here and wait. It's got to happen now. I can't have the army coming into this territory. I'd be ruined. I'd be laughed out of this town. I'd be laughed out of this territory."

Ringo turned his cold flat eyes on the sheriff. He said, "Ya want to rush that ranch house, across the flat plain? You would be in the open for at least half a mile. Do you know what they could do to us with long-range rifles?"

Behan said, "Well, then you can damn well count me out. I'm taking those badges and I'm going back to Tombstone. I cannot have the army in here. You've gotten me in trouble with the governor, Ringo. This thing started out small, and you have let it get larger and larger. You and Curly Bill. Why in hell couldn't you have just left the Earps alone?"

Ringo said, "Because I don't like the Earps, and people that I don't like, I don't want alive. Do you understand that, Behan? And I'm getting real quick to where I don't like you."

Behan was undaunted. He said, "I don't want to hear that right now, Ringo. What I do want to hear is what are you going to do. Either act now or forget it."

Ringo laughed sharply. He looked off in the distance for a moment. He said, "I can think of one thing to do. I don't know if Wyatt's got the stomach for it or not, but we can give it a try. You and your precious governor are worrying me so much, maybe I'll just do it the way I think is best anyhow. Yeah, now that I think about it, I kinda like it this way. Let me get that son of a bitch in sights all by himself. That'll be fun. I'll make that bastard crawl."

"You're saying that you are going to find some way to get a lone play against Wyatt Earp? It'll never happen. He's not that much of a fool. He's not gonna walk into an ambush."

Wyatt had just walked out of Doc's room, where the gambler and gunman had lapsed back into unconsciousness, when he heard Joe Hooker calling him from the front door. He hurried down the hall and stepped out onto the front porch.

A rider, one of Hooker's cowhands, was sitting there on his horse.

Hooker said, "This man has just come in. I've had him posted about a half mile out. He said there is a man bearing down upon us carrying a white flag. What do you suppose? They want to surrender?"

Wyatt said, "Not very damned likely." He didn't even bother to smile.

He looked at the rider. He said, "Go escort him in. I'll wait right here."

After a few moments Frank McMasters joined Wyatt on the front porch. He said, "How's Doc?"

Wyatt shook his head. "He's having a bad spell. I don't know if he'll come out of this one or not. Hell, I don't know how he's come this far. I'm nearly give out from all that riding around the desert that we've been doing."

McMasters glanced up. He said, "Who are those two men coming?"

Wyatt said, "One of them is one of Hooker's hands and the other one is one of the cowboys under a white flag."

McMasters said, "The hell you say."

They watched as the cowhand peeled off from the red-sashed cowboy and went back to his post. The cowboy came on, loping his horse through the entrance of the ranch.

He came riding into the yard and skidded to a stop. He was a tall, lean specimen with three or four days' worth of whiskers on his face and a mean look around his mouth. He stared at Wyatt Earp for a moment and then at McMasters.

He said, "Hello, McMasters. Ain't you in the wrong place?"

McMasters said, "What do you know about smart? You're dumb enough to follow Ringo and Curly Bill, you ain't very smart."

The cowboy said, "I got a message for you."

Wyatt said, "What's the message?"

The cowboy said, "Ringo wants McMasters to come over to our camp for a parley."

McMasters said, "He didn't figure on all the stink that this is causing, did he? Might be that he's looking to strike a bargain. If so, he probably figures he needs somebody like me, who talks his language. That about it, Jack?"

The cowboy switched his gaze back from Wyatt Earp to Frank McMasters.

He said, "I just carry the messages, Frank, I don't try to figure them out."

"Why Frank? Why McMasters?" Wyatt asked.

The cowboy said, "I just answered you. I don't know. All I was told was to ride over here and see if McMasters"—he paused, looking McMasters up and down—"if McMasters has the stomach to come over and talk to Johnny."

Wyatt said, "You just ride your horse over there fifteen or twenty yards. We'll give you an answer in a minute."

"Suit yourself. I ain't workin' by the hour."

He turned his horse and rode over by the ranch-house

fence. Wyatt turned to McMasters and said, "I don't like it."

McMasters shrugged and said, "What can it hurt? Might as well hear him out. What choice we got?"

Frank McMasters stepped down and walked toward his horse. Wyatt came after him.

"Frank, I think we need to talk about this a little more. I don't think you ought to go up there. Hell, that man is capable of anything."

McMasters put a boot in the stirrup and lifted himself into the saddle. He looked down at Wyatt and said, "I don't see how we got much choice. If we sit here and get attacked, a lot of innocent people are going to get killed. We can't stay here forever. If we string out there on the prairie on those dead horses trying to get through to Tombstone or to fort up, they'll run us down and kill us like dogs. Maybe he really does want to strike a bargain."

Wyatt said, "You don't really trust Johnny Ringo, do you?"

McMasters adjusted his hat and looked down the sight of his revolver. He said, "Well, John Behan is with him. He's supposed to be law. What could happen?"

"I don't trust Behan any further than I trust Ringo, and I don't trust him at all. Frank, I don't think that you ought to be doing this."

"Are you ordering me not to do this, Wyatt?"

Wyatt looked thoughtful for a moment. "No, I can't do that either," he said. "If you feel that this is the thing to do, then all I can do is wish you luck and hope that it works out for the best."

McMasters looked down from his horse and said, "Wyatt, I really don't think I'm riding into trouble, but in case I am, no matter what happens, promise me that you'll see it through to the end. If you don't, I'll curse the day that I ever laid eyes on you."

Then, before Wyatt could answer, Frank McMasters whirled his horse and started him at a hard pace across the yard and out the gate of the ranch.

The cowboy, Jack, spurred his horse and raced after him.

Wyatt stood watching, wondering, guessing. He said softly, "Why does it always have to be the good one?"

Frank McMasters followed the cowboy across the desert prairie, not quite riding even with him. The position of his horse was a sort of symbol that he was not actually with the cowboy.

They hit the slope of the little hill where Johnny Ringo and the rest of the cowboys were camped, the vantage point that they had selected overlooking the Hookers' ranch. The place where Ringo had wanted to make his attack from.

They hit the crown and started through rocks and boulders as they made their way toward the camp. McMasters said, "Is the sheriff still there with them?"

Jack said, "Hell, why don't you wait and find out? You know, McMasters, that you ain't really too popular anymore."

"Well, you can imagine just how much I give a damn about that anymore."

They rode into camp. The men were as rough looking as the country. Ringo rose from a small campfire as he saw them coming. As they rode up he smiled a false smile. He said, "Well, hello there, old friend."

McMasters pulled his horse up and said, "We were never that, Ringo. Not even in the best of days, and this damn sure ain't the best of days."

Ringo said, "I'm sorry to hear you talk like that, Frank. You don't seem real friendly."

"I came up here because you wanted to parley. You got something in mind?"

"Yeah, kinda. I wanted to see if you'd join back up with us."

McMasters laughed. He said, "'You are kidding."

Ringo gave him a hard, flat stare. He said, "How many times have you known me to kid, Frank?"

"You mean that's what you really got me back up here for? To see if I would join back up with you bunch of murdering cutthroats?"

Ringo said, "You're a cowboy, you're a brother to the bone, remember? Why don't you come back? No hard feelings."

McMasters smiled at him bitterly. "And what do I have to do for it, Johnny? Tell you how many men there are at the ranch? Tell you how Wyatt's feeling? Tell you how Doc is doing? What sort of information would you want, Ringo, to let me come back in?"

"Well, there never was much fooling you, was there, Frank?"

"What's the matter, Ringo? You starting to get a little heat from the federal law? You know, now that Wyatt is a marshal, there has been a lot of telegrams flying back and forth between him and the federal authorities. I think you just might be in a little more trouble than you think you are."

"Well, Frank, here you are trying to run my business for me. You know how I feel about that. I'm gonna ask you one more time if you care to come back. Like I said, there will be no hard feelings."

McMasters made a sort of a hoot, somewhere between

scorn and a laugh. He said, "Forget it, Ringo. I wouldn't join you for a key to Fort Knox and all the most beautiful women in the world."

Behind him, one of the cowboys said, "Why do you keep fooling with him, Johnny? Hell, why don't you jerk him off that horse and stick a knife to his throat and then see how he talks."

Ringo looked around. "Next one of you son of a bitches that opens your mouth, I'm liable to see how you talk with a bullet hole in your head."

He turned back to Frank McMasters. He said, "Isn't there anything I can say to make you change your mind? Or are you going to stay with your new friends?"

McMasters looked down at him from atop his horse and said, "At least they don't scare women."

"Well, if you're talking about that stagecoach, I had nothing to do with that."

"You may not have had anything personally to do about it; Fuller and his partner got off on their own. But you're the example of what they done, Johnny. You'd have done it yourself if you'd had the chance."

Ringo looked at him and said, "There ain't no need for this harsh talk, Frank. Why don't you step down from your horse and have a cup of coffee. Let's talk this thing over."

"I guess your hearing is going, Johnny. I done told you three times, no. How many more times is it going to take?"

Ringo looked up at him and sighed. An evil, flat smile flickered across his face. He said, "Well, you're the boss. But there is one thing, though." He took a few steps closer until he was standing right beside Frank McMaster's horse.

He looked up at him. McMasters said, "And what would that one thing be?"

"Oh, I was just wondering how you were going to get back to your friends?"

McMasters said, "So, it's going to be like that, huh? Your word ain't no better than it ever was. Well, I guess it's just as well that I ain't surprised. The shock might have killed me. But I might be a little harder to take than you think."

With a sudden move, his hand started toward his gun. But before he could reach it, the cowboy who was still on his horse, Jack, leaped from his saddle, tackling McMasters around the shoulder, bringing him down to the ground. As he did, the cowboys rushed forward and subdued Frank McMasters.

But his trouble was short-lived. In a moment Frank was pinned down to the ground. He looked up at Johnny Ringo and said, "Well, what do you plan to do now, Johnny? Are you just gonna kill me out of hand, or are you going to give me a fighting chance?"

Ringo said, "Get some ropes. Tie one rope to each hand, long ropes. And a rope to each leg. And pump that fire up real good, get it burning real good. Then let it burn down to hot coals."

A little fear entered the brave eyes of Frank McMasters. He said, "What do you have in mind, Johnny?"

Ringo, his flat dead eyes almost showing life at the prospect, said, "We're going to do a little cooking, Frank."

"What kind of cooking?"

Ringo said, "Well, let us just get the pot ready first."

With the fear surging through him, giving him strength, McMasters struggled hard as the other cowboys were trying to rope each of his hands and each of his feet. Once he almost succeeded in breaking away, but then one of the cowboys drove his fist hard into Frank's stomach, taking his breath away.

Ringo said, "Gently there, Bob. We don't want to bruise the meat."

Frank McMasters looked frightened. He said, "All right, Ringo, you've had your fun. If you're gonna kill me, get on with it, you dirty son of a bitch. But rest assured of one thing, though. Wyatt Earp is going to get you before this is all over."

Ringo said, "Oh, I don't think Wyatt Earp is going to get anybody. But we're gonna have some fun with you first. Are you about ready for some late lunch?"

McMasters said, "What are you planning, Johnny?"

"Well, I thought we would have a barbecue."

"Yeah?" asked McMasters.

Johnny Ringo gave him that hard flat look. He said, "Yeah, I figured we'd barbecue and you're about the handiest thing."

He turned to the other cowboys and said, "Boys, get those ropes and let's stretch our friend here out over the fire and warm his bones up."

As they lifted him up into position, a cowboy on each rope, he rose up off the ground, spread eagle. Frank McMasters swore to himself that he would not scream.

It was not a vow that he could keep.

It was late at night when the cowboy named Jack came riding back to the Hooker ranch. One of the sentinel picked him up about a half mile out from the ranch headquarters and escorted him back to the house. He was leading a horse with a blanket-wrapped load of some kind.

They came into the yard and the Hooker rider let out a yell to summon those inside. Jack stood there, sitting on his horse, waiting as Wyatt, Joe Hooker, Turkey Johnson, and Vermillion stepped out onto the porch, holding lanterns aloft. He pulled the lead horse up to the porch and dismounted. He went to the horse that carried the bundle, untied it, and flopped it down to the ground. It landed heavily. Then he mounted his own horse and backed away.

Wyatt and Jack Vermillion, holding their lanterns nigh, stepped off the porch and walked over to the blanket-wrapped object. Wyatt bent down and lifted back just enough of the flap to see what was inside. He lifted his eyes away from the charred and burned corpse. He felt almost sick to his stomach.

He said, "Oh hell. Oh hell and damnation. My God, Frank, what have they done to you?"

Vermillion said, "Why couldn't they have just killed him? Why did they have to do this? My God, look what they did to him. And he was a good man."

Wyatt looked at the cowboy and asked, "What is this supposed to mean?"

The cowboy sat his horse ten yards away. He said, "Ringo said that he wanted to be sure he got your attention, Marshal. Does this do it?"

Wyatt said, "It gets my attention all right, and a little more."

"Ringo wants a straight-up fight, just you and him. Settle this thing, once and for all. If you win, we quit the territory. If Ringo wins, your deputies get safe conduct to the Colorado line. He don't think you've got the stomach for it. He wants to meet you at Oak Grove at the mouth of Sulphur Springs Canyon. You know the place?"

Wyatt said, "Yeah, I know the place."

"What do you want me to tell Ringo?"

"You tell him that I'll be there. You tell him that I don't expect that he's got the stomach to face me alone. You tell him that I said I expect to be walking into an ambush. But tell him that his ambush just might not work. But if he's there alone, he'll get fair play from me."

Jack laughed. "Ringo said you'd say something like that. He wants you to know that he don't need no help with you. He don't think you've got a chance. That's the reason that he don't think you'll show."

Wyatt said, "What time?"

"Tomorrow morning. Seven A.M. That give you enough time to say your prayers?"

Jack Vermillion suddenly said, "Let me kill this son of bitch. He had a hand in it. At least let me kill this one."

He drew his revolver.

Wyatt put out his hand. He said, "No. He's got to carry word back to Ringo." He looked at Jack. "You tell him that I'll be there. Tell him I'm looking forward to it. Now get out of here before I change my mind and shoot you myself."

Jack let out a wild laugh and reeled his horse and rode away. Then they looked down at the charred remains of Frank McMasters. Joe Hooker came up. Wyatt said, "Joe, can we bury him on your place? This is honest soil. I think that this is where he would like to be buried."

Hooker said, "Sure, Wyatt. Let's get some shovels. I hate this, God, I hate this country sometimes."

Wyatt said, "It's not the country, Joe. Ringo would be Ringo no matter where he was. Any kind of country."

They turned and started toward the barn. As they walked Wyatt said, "I should have never let him go. I should have never let him go by himself."

Turkey Johnson said, "Wyatt, you couldn't have stopped him. Don't blame yourself for this. It's not your fault."

They buried McMasters at about two o'clock in the morning. Mrs. Hooker came out, dressed in her flannel robe.

She brought her Bible and said a few words. They were a little more comforted by it.

When they patted down the last spade full of dirt on the fresh grave, they put the shovels away and went into the ranch parlor.

Mrs. Hooker ran to the kitchen to put on a pot of fresh coffee.

Jack Vermillion said, "I don't know about yall, but I could do with a drink."

Johnson said, "Why don't you just pour us all out a round and quit talking about it?"

After they had drinks in their hands and a few sips had been taken, Turkey Johnson said, "Wyatt, I don't think you ought to go up and meet Johnny Ringo. Are you crazy?"

Jack said, "It's not finished. It won't mean nothing by this, and God knows that I'm nobody to tell you anything to be telling you about courage or about skill with a gun or about smarts. But Wyatt, you can't beat him. I've seen him in action. He's the fastest thing that I've ever seen. I'm not sure that Doc Holliday could even beat him. God knows, you're good and you've got more courage than the old rip himself, but you ain't in Ringo's class. Hell, he's the best that's ever been. 'Cept for maybe Wild Bill. I don't know."

Turkey Johnson said, "He's right, Wyatt. You're a lawman. You don't have to go up against a mad-dog killer like that. Listen, Ringo could put five into you before you could even get off one in him."

Wyatt took a long drink of whiskey. He said, "But I'd do it. If I could just get that one into him, so help me God, I'd be willing to take the five in me."

Turkey Johnson and Vermillion just stared at him. Finally, Turkey said, "All right, Wyatt, maybe you can. Hell, you've done more for this territory than any man I've ever seen. But you've gotta die to do it. You gotta die."

The words came like lead bullets striking Wyatt. The expression on his face slowly changed to one of misery and grim resignation as he realized that both Johnson and Vermillion were right.

Five miles from the Hooker ranch was the greenest place in that part of the Arizona Territory. There was a large oak grove that grew up from a creek. It had been there forever, some of the oaks were over twenty feet high. They looked strange in that part of the country. They covered almost ten acres of ground, fed by the creek that forked on both sides of it. There was even lush green beneath the canopy of leaves. It was an odd place to choose for a duel to the death.

Johnny Ringo came riding into the grove with the two other cowboys. He dismounted his horse beside the shade of the biggest oak.

He said to the men waiting nearby, "As soon as I'm through with Wyatt, I want you to finish off Turkey Jack Johnson and Jack Vermillion. I want you to burn them all."

Ike Clanton was one of the two men that accompanied Ringo. He said, "I bet he ain't even going to show."

Ringo said, "Ike, you never were very smart, you're not good with a gun, you're a coward and a loudmouth, so how would you even know anything about a man like Wyatt Earp? Matter of fact, how've you managed to stay alive this long? Now you get the hell out of here and go with the rest of them."

Ike said, "You sure you don't want us to bushwhack him?"

Ringo said, "You don't know anything, do you, Clanton?

Wyatt Earp will show and I will take care of him. Personally. Now get."

As the two cowboys rode off, Ringo flipped open the loading gate of his pistol and reached to the back of his belt for a .45-caliber cartridge. He carefully loaded all six chambers and leaned up against the oak to wait.

Sunrise came early in the Western desert during the summer. It has been light, good light, since six A.M. Johnny Ringo got his watch out and noticed that it was just past six-thirty.

He had come to the oak grove early, deliberately. Even though he had declared that he wanted a facedown with Wyatt Earp, he had no intention of keeping his word. He was fairly certain he could beat Earp in a fair contest. But Johnny Ringo was not a man to leave anything to chance or to leave himself exposed to any unnecessary danger.

Consequently, he was going to make certain that Wyatt Earp would never have the chance to draw, much less leave the grove of oak trees alive.

Ringo had positioned himself at the far eastern end of the trees. He would hear Earp coming a long time before Wyatt would be aware of his presence. It would look like a fair fight to those who came later, but it wasn't going to be one.

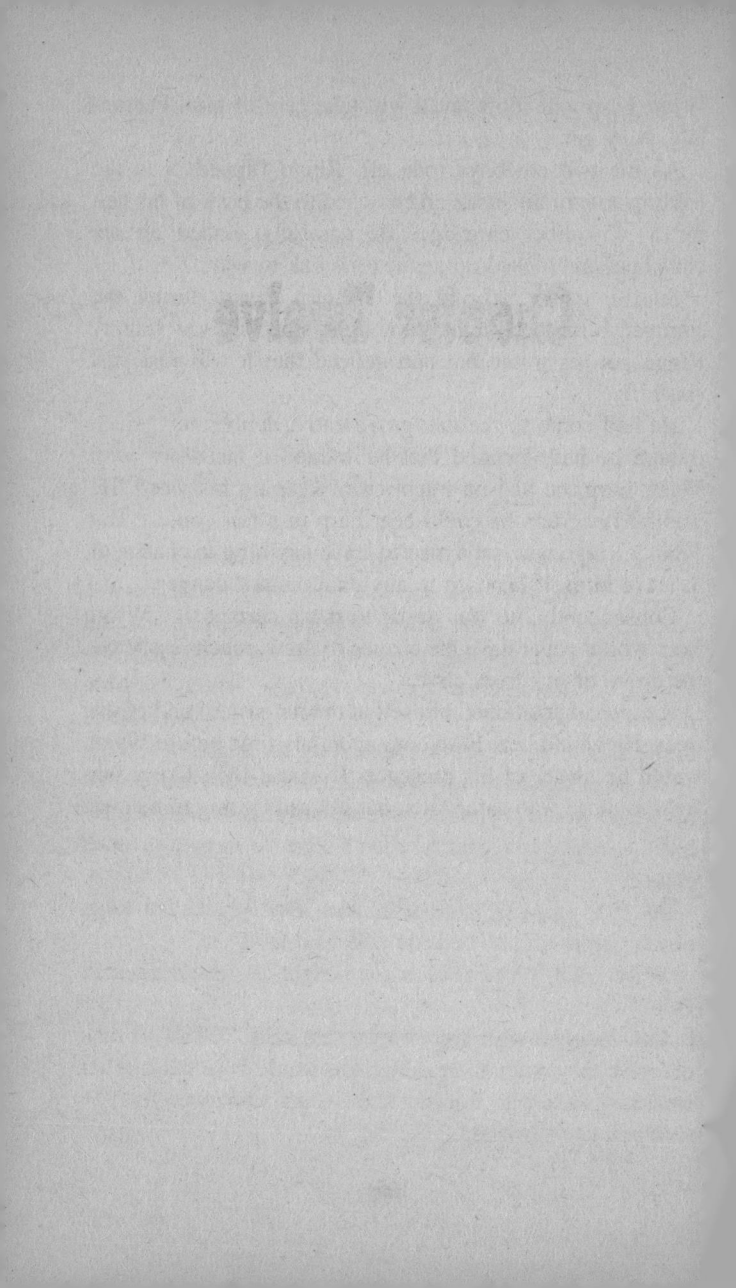

Chapter Twelve

Doc had rallied and woke up about four in the morning. He still looked frail and wan and very, very weak. He was propped up against the pillow, drinking whiskey. He and Wyatt had been talking for about half an hour. Doc was sipping at his whiskey like it was medicine, which, for him, it was. The numbing effect soothed his lungs and softened the racking cough that took him every so often.

Wyatt looked at him with concern. He wasn't certain that his friend would last much more than twenty-four hours. He hated to leave him, but he didn't seem to have too much choice.

As if to make a liar out of him, Doc plucked a long, slender cigar off the bedside table and lit it.

Wyatt said, "You reckon you ought to be doing that, Doc?"

Doc laughed with hollow eyes. He said, "Wyatt, if men did what they ought to be doing, this would be a much better world, wouldn't it? But that's not going to happen, is it?"

Wyatt just shrugged.

Doc said, "You know, it's funny the place that Johnny Ringo chose to have it out in. Did you know that that grove of trees was where they used to hold camp meetings and preachings before Tombstone got built and got some churches? Kinda funny, ain't it?"

Wyatt said grimly, "I don't think it's the kind of ground that will be of much use for preaching after what happens today."

He paused. Then he said earnestly, "Doc, I guess I'm a little too old to be asking that question. But somehow, you seem to see more things than most men. I want to know what you think makes a man like Ringo, Doc, what makes him do the things he does?"

Doc cleared his throat. He said, "A man like Ringo has a great big empty hole right through the middle of him, and no matter what he does, he can't ever fill it. He can't kill enough, steal enough, or inflict enough pain to ever fill it. And it drives him mad, crazy mad, sick mad. He's cold and dirty inside. He's a swamp inside, Wyatt."

Wyatt said, "So what does he want?"

"What does he want? He wants revenge."

"Revenge? For what?"

Doc looked at him with a look of pure sadness in his sunken eyes. He said simply. "For being born."

Wyatt looked down and looked at his boot tops for a minute. There didn't seem to be a lot to say after what Doc had just explained. He took the bottle of whiskey off the nightstand and had a long sip straight out of the bottle. He set it down.

He said, "Doc, do you remember how I said it all happened so fast with Curly Bill, that I didn't have time to think about it? Yall seemed to think it was some sort of miracle. It wasn't. I just didn't know what I was doing. Well,

I've had plenty of time to think about this. This business of facing Johnny Ringo. You know, I spent most of my life since I was born not knowing what I wanted out of life, just chasing my tail. But now, for the first time in my life, I know just what I want, and who. That's the misery of it. I can't have it."

He paused and looked deep into Doc's eyes. He said, "I can't beat him, can I, Doc?"

Doc slowly shook his head sadly. Wyatt looked at him for a second longer and nodded his head in resignation and then got up, ready to leave. He said, "Well, I guess I had better get kicking."

Doc said, "No, wait. I'm going with you."

He struggled to sit up, the effort leaving him trembling and sweating. Wyatt put out a hand and gently pushed him back down.

Wyatt said, "Thanks, Doc, but this one is for me."

Doc said, "I'm sorry, Wyatt."

A sudden spasm of coughing took Doc Holliday and it was half a minute before he could speak again. He said, "I'm sorry, Wyatt. God, I'm sorry."

Wyatt said, "That's all right, Doc. I don't want you to worry. I just want you to rest and get well."

Doc put out his trembling hand and pointed to Wyatt's United States marshal's badge. He said, "I never got to wear one of those. You swore us in, but you never had no badges to give us."

Wyatt smiled slowly. He took his badge off, but before he handed it to Doc, he said, "Doc, you've never needed a badge. You've always been straight inside and that's what counts. It's not the badge that makes a man straight, but what he's got inside him."

Doc smiled and said, "Much more of that kind of talk and I'll have to sob into my hankie."

Wyatt smiled again and took his badge and pressed it into Doc's palm. Doc's hand closed around it. He smiled and then laid his head back up on the pillow, his eyes closed.

Wyatt took one last look at him and then turned and left the room.

It was growing late to make the rendezvous on time. Wyatt stepped out onto the porch where Hooker and the others were waiting. He directed a look at Joe Hooker.

The rancher said, "Don't worry about Doc. Mrs. Hooker will give him the best care that he'll get anywhere. And if they want him, they'll have to go through me and my men first."

Wyatt nodded gratefully and then offered his hand. Hooker took it and they shook. He said, "Good luck, Wyatt. Not that I think you'll need it."

Wyatt stepped off the porch again and joined Johnson and Vermillion. Together they mounted up and rode out of the ranch through the gate, kicking their horses up into a slow gallop.

In the clear morning light, they could see the little rise studded with oak trees, set amid the forks of Sulphur Creek, that gave the canyon and the grove its name. To Wyatt's eyes, it looked frighteningly close.

Even though he knew he was running late, Wyatt set a deliberately slow pace. His friends noticed it, but made no remarks. They could understand his reluctance. They did not mistake it for fear or cowardice. They thought it was only the conscious act of a man approaching a very grave confrontation that was going to take all his will and strength.

To them, Wyatt had nothing to prove. He had saved their lives on many occasions, risking his own in the bargain. He had gone through hellfire and lived. Now they hated that his pride would not let him turn aside from what was almost certain doom.

Jack Vermillion said with a try at false cheerfulness, "Nice morning, ain't it?"

No one answered him. Wyatt glanced to his right. Off to the south, perhaps a mile or two away, he could see a horseman, running his horse hard. He was heading southeast.

Wyatt said, "Wonder who the hell that could be?"

Turkey Creek Johnson said, "Reckon that's Johnny Ringo running a little late?"

Wyatt chuckled a little. He said, "I doubt it."

Johnson said, "Maybe it's one of his lookouts heading to warn him that you're on your way."

Wyatt shook his head. He said, "The man doesn't appear to be heading for the Sulphur Springs oak grove. He's heading too far south. Unless he means to circle around him and come up from the end or the side. He ain't going that way. Hell, maybe it's just some honest cowboy headed for a day's work." He laughed dryly, "It seems like the way our lives have been going lately that we've forgotten about the ordinary work. That there really is some kind of life other than hunting and being hunted, and chasing and being chased, and killing and being killed."

Johnson and Vermillion looked at each other and shook their heads sadly. There wasn't a word that they could reply to that. They rode on.

A half mile from the entrance of the canyon at Sulphur Springs, Wyatt pulled his horse up. The others followed suit.

Wyatt said, "You know that Johnny Ringo is lying about giving you two and Doc safe passage out of this territory. I don't want you to stay around here. As soon as the shooting starts, I want you to go back and ask Doc if he can travel and head east for the New Mexico line. I don't want you—"

Jack Vermillion quickly said, "Wyatt, I'm just not going to do that. I am going in that thicket of woods with you."

Jack Johnson said, "And so am I. Wyatt, you know that son of a bitch probably has an ambush set in there for you. There is no way that we're going to let you go in there by yourself."

Wyatt looked at both of them. He said, "Maybe he does have an ambush. Is it better for three of us to be caught in it than one?"

Jack Vermillion protested, "That ain't the point. We are not letting you go in alone."

Wyatt smiled slowly. He said, "Well, boys. I've got a hole card that you haven't seen yet, which gives me the winning hand. Remember that you swore an oath as deputy marshals? Well, I'm your boss. I'm not asking you to leave, I'm *ordering* you to leave. Now, you boys wouldn't want to break a federal law by disobeying the order of your boss, now, would you?"

They stared at him. Turkey Creek Johnson said, "Aw, hell, Wyatt. That ain't fair."

Wyatt said, "I don't mean for it to be."

Vermillion said, "You can't order us to do that, Wyatt. Hell, I quit."

Wyatt shook his head, still smiling. He said, "I'm asking you as a friend. Please, go back and take care of Doc. I'll see you within an hour."

They didn't believe him, but he had asked them as a friend, which left them with no choice. In an awkward gesture, they both stuck out their hands at the same time. Their horses crowded close to Wyatt's. In turn, he shook each man's hand gravely.

Johnson said, "Wyatt, I . . ." He almost choked. "I ain't got the words, dammit."

Wyatt said, "Me neither."

He patted Johnson on the shoulder and then gave Vermillion a little salute and said, "Now take off boys."

He watched as they turned their horses and started off at a slow trot. They glanced back once. He waved. Resolutely, they faced forward toward Hooker's ranch. Finally, they kicked their horses up into a slow gallop. Only then did Wyatt urge his horse forward to enter the wide opening of the canyon and was under the spreading shade of the oak trees.

He dismounted and tied his horse to a handy limb. Then slowly he began to walk toward the center of the grove. Behind him, his horse neighed as if in farewell. Wyatt looked back and smiled. It was a gorgeous morning. The sun dappled through the newly leafed oaks, making shadows and light dance upon the ground. Wyatt continued along the trail, walking slowly, seeming to drink in all the light that he could, all the light that surrounded him. He was like a man grasping at what time he had left.

Then suddenly he closed his eyes and fell to his knees, trembling. He was truly afraid for the first time in his life. He clasped his hands and looked up through the bower of leaves and branches.

"Dear Lord, this is the last battle. I worked it out in my head every which way, and I know there is no way I'm coming through this alive. For whatever reason, you've preserved me this far. Maybe it was for this. So I'll only ask one favor. Just let me live long enough to take care of this man so that he can never again hurt another soul."

Wyatt paused. He said, "Thy will be done, and there is an amen to it."

Wyatt stood up. He could feel the fear draining out of him. Now with determination in his heart for his meeting with the man he was almost certain would kill him, either by fair or foul means. As he walked the music of his spurs trailed him, going *ching, ching, ching.*

Johnny Ringo stood in the little clearing in the midst of the oaks leaning against a tree, sipping from a hip flask and smoking a slim cigar. Around him, the canopy of leaves made it as dark as evening in their midst. But the sun was clear and bright in the small clearing.

Ringo smoked quietly, occasionally moving his head to look first to the right and then to the left.

Faintly, he could hear the *ching, ching, ching* of spurs approaching. He looked quickly to his left through the thicket of tree trunks. He could see the slim silhouette flitting from shadow to shadow. He dropped the cigar and pushed the flask into his pocket and stepped away from the tree.

To the silhouette coming closer he said, "Well, I didn't think you had it in you." He smiled and set himself. "Well, shall we have it?"

The silhouette was almost to the edge of the clearing. The voice sounded loud and clear. The words were, "I'm your huckleberry."

Ringo stiffened as the silhouette stepped into the clearing and became Doc Holliday. It was a pale, drawn, and weak-looking Doc, but he was awake and ready for game.

Ringo said, "What the hell are you doing here, Holliday?"

Doc smiled, his lips twisting cynically. "Well, Johnny Ringo, you look like somebody just walked over your grave." He laughed. "And maybe they will pretty quick. Oh,

I wasn't quite as sick as I made out, and besides, you and I have some unfinished business and I wouldn't want to miss that."

Ringo said, "My fight's not with you, Holliday."

"I beg to differ. We started a fight that we never got to finish. Play for blood, remember?"

Ringo said, "I was kidding about that."

A twisted smile came over Doc's face. He said, "I wasn't."

He pulled his coat back to reveal where he had pinned Wyatt's badge to his jacket. He said, "And this time, it is legal. Think what a treat that will be for me. To actually kill a cur dog like you in the name of the law."

Ringo's eyes went dead. His shock had now been replaced by a growing malice. As they set into each other, once again, their eyes began to blaze, boring into each other, about to explode.

Ringo said, "All right, lunger, let's do it. That is, if you can stand long enough."

Doc said, "You call it."

For a long tense moment, they stared at one another. Then there was a sudden blurred moment as they both drew at the same time. Only one shot rang out.

Ringo stumbled backward, a bullet hole slanting through the upper part of his chest. Doc slapped his gun back in his holster.

Back in the thicket, Wyatt heard the gunshot. He started running; he couldn't understand it.

With blood coursing from the mortal wound in his chest, Ringo stumbled sideways in jerks and starts. The pistol still in his hand.

Doc stepped closer and danced in front of him, urging

him on. "Come on, come on, boy. Shoot that iron. Use it for what it was intended for."

But there was no shot. Ringo's pistol never reached firing position. His arm fell to his side and then he slumped sideways into the crook of an oak tree, his pistol hitting the ground as he fell against the tree.

Doc took two steps forward and looked down at him. He said, "Oh Johnny, you're no daisy, no daisy at all."

At the sound behind him, Doc whirled to see Wyatt appear in the clearing. They stared at each other. Surprise was on Wyatt's face.

Wyatt said, "What the hell are *you* doing here?"

Doc said, "This was my fight to finish."

For the first time Wyatt noticed the badge on Doc Holliday's chest. "So that is why you wanted the badge. So you could kill a man as a marshal. What am I supposed to say?"

Doc shrugged. "Well, you might offer to buy me a drink."

Wyatt laughed in spite of himself. He said, "Doc, you are the daisy. You're the one and only daisy."

Doc said, "It was my pleasure, sir. I enjoyed being a marshal. I think I'll give you your badge back now that we are finished."

Wyatt said, "We're not finished yet. Johnny Ringo was just the head of the snake. We've still got the rest of it to kill."

Nestled atop a low, flat mesa, the rest of the cowboys now led by Sheriff John Behan sat and waited for the return of Johnny Ringo and the two men he had taken with him. Up on the rock-strewn mesa, a cowboy had climbed atop one of the larger boulders. In the distance, he could see dust and then he yelled down to the others, "Riders coming."

Behan and the other cowboys got up from where they had been taking their ease on the ground. Behan had been drinking from a bottle of brandy. He smiled as he thought of what had now happened to Wyatt Earp and his friends. They had been a constant nuisance to him, one that he was glad to get rid of.

There was a small twinge of conscience as he thought about what had been done to Frank McMasters, but he held no grief for Wyatt Earp or the others, especially Doc Holliday. They had insulted him, demeaned him, they had made him look small in the eyes of the townspeople, and John Behan was a vain man, too vain to tolerate such treatment.

Behan yelled up to the cowboy on the rock. He said, "How close are they?"

The cowboy said, "Oh, I reckon about half a mile. But there is four of them. I don't quite understand that. What'd ya reckon, Sheriff?"

Behan shrugged and said, "I don't know. They might have picked up someone that had wondered off."

In the camp, only about fifteen cowboys remained. The rest had either been killed or had deserted, but Behan had plans to build the group again. With the help of Johnny Ringo, he knew that it would be an easy task.

Out in the desert, coming hard, was not Johnny Ringo and three outlaws. Instead, it was Wyatt Earp, Doc Holliday, Turkey Johnson, and Jack Vermillion. They hurtled across the plains, at top speed, their horses eating up the distance. They were two hundred yards away and then they were only one hundred yards away.

They had ridden with shotguns at the ready across the pummels of their saddles.

Suddenly the cowboy up above recognized them. He yelled, "Hell, it ain't Ringo at all. It's the Earp bunch. My God, it's that damned Wyatt Earp and that damned Doc Holliday, and them others."

John Behan said, "Oh no. Oh, hell no. What the hell could have happened to Johnny?"

Behan began to panic. Sour, heavy, churning acid rose in his stomach. The cowboy on the rock jumped down and mounted his horse.

John Behan said, "Where the hell do you think you're going?"

The cowboy said, "I think it's time to start working for a living. I'm getting the hell out of here."

Behan stared at him for a minute. Then he said, "Me too."

With a bound he was on his horse, following the cowboy as he streaked in the opposite direction from the approaching lawmen.

Panic spread like wildfire through the remaining men. As rapidly as they could, they mounted their horses and began trying to race away in all directions. Only Ike Clanton stood his ground. He looked around, screaming at them, beside himself as they all rode away.

He screamed, "Wait, dammit, wait. Why don't you kill 'em? Kill 'em. It's only four men. Why don't you kill 'em."

A passing cowboy yelled back, "You kill 'em."

They were scattered like sparks from a blazing fire, going in every direction. Ike watched them for a second, and in that second, Wyatt Earp and his three deputies crested the rim of the mesa and bore down straight into the camp.

Ike started running. As fast as he could, he slung into the saddle of his horse and started spurring him on. Wyatt and his men kept coming at a full gallop, firing their guns. First one cowboy then another fell out of their saddle as the buckshot took its toll.

Then they crested the rise from the other side of the mesa, the ground seeming to fall out from under them. For a moment they appeared almost airborne, grim-faced avenging angels on winged horses. Now even more majestic in the gathering twilight, like a myth made flesh, awesome, superb, unstoppable. In that instant, Wyatt Earp had found vindication. He had found justification. He had found fulfillment.

What few remaining cowboys were left were scattering in all directions. They would never again gather as a group.

John Behan knew that he was finished in southeastern Arizona. He fled south, afraid to look back. His goal was Mexico and at least temporary safety.

Wyatt put up his hand and slowed his horse gradually as the others followed suit. Finally, they came to a stop. They were surrounded by empty desert and clear skies above. Only in the distance could they see the occasional dust of a fleeing cowboy.

Wyatt turned slowly to each man and shook his hand. He said, "It's finished. We did our job and I thank you."

Chapter Fourteen

Chapter Thirteen

The clock on the wall in the private Denver hospital ticked gently but inexorably as Doc lay peacefully in bed, with Father Feeney, a Catholic priest, at his side. Doc was drawn and gaunt, emaciated, his breathing shallow and labored. He was so weak that it was all he could do even to move his eyes, but they brightened as Wyatt entered the room.

Doc said in a horse whisper, "Well, hello, Wyatt. Father Feeney's just been initiating me into the mysteries of the great and ancient Church of Rome. You see, it appears that my hypocrisy knows no bounds."

Wyatt tried to hide his sick feeling inside, said, "How're ya doin', Doc?"

Doc tried for a hoarse chuckle, but it came out more rasp. He said, "Rather an obvious question under the circumstances, don't you agree? A better one might be, 'How do you feel?'"

Wyatt shook his head and laughed a little.

Doc said, "So now we can add self-pity to your list of frailties."

With supreme effort, Doc Holliday lifted up his hand and held it out to Wyatt. Resting in his palm was the badge that he had taken so long ago on that day when he had gone to kill Johnny Ringo for Wyatt.

Doc said, "I just wanted to see what it felt like. Here."

He tried to hand it back, but Wyatt stopped him, pressing his palm onto the badge and guiding it over Doc's heart.

Doc gasped and coughed for a moment and then, when he could, he said, "You're the most fallible, wrongheaded, self-deluding, just generally benighted jackass I've ever known." He stopped for a moment to get enough breath to go on. "Yet, withal, even at your worst, you're the only human being in my entire life who ever gave me hope."

Wyatt could feel tears welling up in his eyes. He said, "All I ever wanted to do is live a normal life."

Doc said, "You wouldn't know a normal life if it bit you in the ass."

Wyatt smiled. "That's great coming from you."

"I played the cards that I was dealt, Wyatt. Your problem is that you're always trying to play someone else's. Allow me to thus set you free. There is no happiness, Wyatt. There is no normal life. Just life, that's all. Grab that black-haired woman and make her your own. Run and don't look back. Live every second, live it right up to the hilt. Live, Wyatt. . . ."

He paused and reached for Wyatt's hand.

For a second they remained like that, their eyes locked, their hands joined.

Doc said, "Live for me."

Wyatt stared into his eyes, letting the thought sink in. Just then Doc looked up as if someone were pressing on him. He said in a faltering voice, "Wyatt, please, if you were ever my friend, if you ever had even the smallest feeling for me, leave me now, please."

Wyatt started to speak, but Doc raised a frail hand to him.

Doc said, "Never mind, Wyatt. I know. I feel the same way."

Doc turned his face away. Slowly Wyatt started backing toward the door. With one hand on the door, he nodded at Doc. A nod of approval. Barely able to move, Doc returned the compliment.

Wyatt went out the door, closing it softly behind him.

With the last of his breath, Doc Holliday said, "Father, you had better start the ball rolling."

Father Feeney nodded and picked up his missal. As he started to intone the last rites Doc looked down at the end of his bed and saw his feet poking through the sheets. He smiled.

"I'll be damned," he said. He looked at Father Feeney and said, "Don't you think that's funny?"

The priest said, "I don't understand, Mr. Holliday."

Doc tried to laugh, but he didn't have the breath for it. He said, "I don't have my boots on."

It was late night in the theater. The performance had been over for half an hour. Back in the dressing room, three actresses were dressing up, dressing for the street, in daring frocks with plunging necklines. They were all in good spirits as they said good night and good luck to each other.

Soon the dressing room was empty except for Josephine Marcus. She sat in preoccupied lethargy, still dressed in her stage clothes. She stared at her reflection in the mirror.

A sudden voice startled her. The voice said, "Did you ever see the sun come up over the Rockies?"

Josephine slowly turned toward the doorway. Wyatt Earp stood there, smiling.

He said, "That sun hits all of a sudden, and below, there's California." He walked straight to her. "And you swear that you are looking at heaven."

She rose slowly, hardly able to believe her eyes. For a second they simply embraced, holding each other close. Wyatt began to smother her with kisses, first on the mouth, then her nose, then her eyes, her forehead, and then a long lingering kiss on her mouth before he pulled his head back.

He said, "I have nothing left. I have nothing to give you. I have no pride, no dignity, no money. I don't even know how we'll make a living. But I promise you that I will love you every second of your life."

She looked up into his face, stroking his cheek as if to make sure that he was really there.

She said, in a saucy way, "Don't worry. My family's rich."

Wyatt said. "Yeah, so is mine."

Josephine laughed and grabbed her coat. She said, "Let's get out of here. Let's go some place where we can be alone. Very alone together. Very much alone."

Together they hurried out of the dressing room. She was too much in love to bother with the fact that she hadn't changed her clothes.

As they were rushing out of the theater a reporter recognized Wyatt. He couldn't believe his good luck—a big story right in front of him. The reporter stepped forward.

He said, "Mr. Earp. Mr. Earp, just one minute, please."

Suddenly Wyatt and Josephine were nearly swarmed by other reporters. They hunched down and ducked through the side door.

A theater employee told the reporters to leave, then

tugged on a reporter's sleeve. He said, "What's the commotion? Who are they?"

"Don't you know? That's Wyatt Earp, the Lion of Tombstone, and his lady fair."

Outside, it was snowing, but Wyatt and Josephine, aware only of each, didn't notice. They ran along the slippery boardwalk, laughing and sliding.

Wyatt pulled her close, clasping her hands in his. They stopped and he pulled her to him.

He said, "I promise, I swear, I'll love you every second of your life."

Josephine looked up into his eyes and said, "You better."

They embraced, seeming to melt into one person. Wyatt had finally found his happiness. Doc had been wrong.

Epilogue

That there was a boomtown called Tombstone, there is no doubt. That there was gunfight at the O.K. Corral, there is also no doubt.

Whether or not it was more important or more historically interesting than any one of the many other gunfights is open to question. Probably its fascination down through the years has been because it involved the charismatic presence and force of Wyatt Earp.

The account given here is as true as research can make it, but it must be remembered that in those days, communication was vague and uncertain. Reports of such incidents as the gunfight at the O.K. Corral were often weeks behind their actual happening.

Eyewitness reports of this celebrated gunfight even varied from newspaper to newspaper. As much as a year later, controversy raged: as to exactly what was its cause, exactly how it took place, and exactly how it ended. There could be no doubt as to who died or who was shot. That was a matter of public record.

Also on record is that after the coming of the Earps and after their time in the town and the territory surrounding Tombstone, the thefts, the murders, and the brutal bullying of innocent people stopped.

If Wyatt Earp and his brothers didn't cause that change, then who did? Certainly not Sheriff Behan and his covey of crooked deputies, or any of the town marshals that the townspeople frantically appointed. No, it had to be the Earps, with Wyatt in the lead, reluctantly picking up a gun again and bringing law and order to a badly uncivilized and desperately dangerous place.

Curiously enough, the loudmouthed bully and coward, Ike Clanton, who had so much to do with the events that led to the gunfight at the O.K. Corral, escaped the wrath of Virgil and of Morgan and of Wyatt. He was finally killed in 1887 by an unknown deputy while in the process of stealing horses.

Doc Holliday died after the shootout of tuberculosis in a Denver hospital.

Sadly enough, Mattie Earp was hell-bent on self-destruction. Wyatt Earp did finally leave her, but it was almost a full year after he had fallen in love with Josephine Marcus. He saw her through many trying times, but in 1886, she succumbed to illnesses that were the result of heroin usage. Of course, Morgan died in 1882, mainly at the hands of Frank Stillwell, who was later killed by Wyatt Earp.

Virgil, though crippled by the shotgun blast in his side, managed to live until 1906, when, as a result perhaps of weakened lungs caused by the gunshots, he died of pneumonia.

Wyatt and Josephine led a life together that can only be described as splendid and satisfying. After Wyatt left law enforcement and found Josephine, still on stage, they were married and embarked on a series of adventures throughout the West. They made and lost several fortunes, but they always led the high life, spending every winter, just the two of them, prospecting for gold in the desert hills of southern California. For forty-seven years, up or down, thin or thick, they never left each other's side.

Wyatt Earp settled in what is now known as Hollywood, California, a fitting place for a man of such large dreams. A man bigger than life. He died there in 1929, a friend to many of the Western film stars of the day. Among the pallbearers at his funeral were Western movie stars William S. Hart and Tom Mix.

They say that Tom Mix wept.